## "Let the rest of the world think we're a love match."

Joss added. "There's just one thing, though...." His fingers caught Nell's wrist. "At the moment, we'd never convince anyone that we're in love. Lovers carry with them an aura of intimacy. Lovers touch and kiss."

Imperceptibly, he had drawn her closer to him, and Nell trembled.

"It's all right, Nell, I'm only going to kiss you. Don't act like a little girl obliged to kiss a much-disliked relative."

His head bent toward her, and Nell quivered tensely, willing herself not to behave like a complete fool by showing how deeply she cared for him.

Joss misunderstood. "Poor Nell," he taunted. "There's no need to look so terrified." And then his mouth was on hers—and all her senses came alive....

**PENNY JORDAN** was constantly in trouble in school because of her inability to stop daydreaming—especially during French lessons. In her teens she was an avid romance reader, although it didn't occur to her to try writing one herself until she was older. "My first half-dozen attempts ended up ingloriously," she remembers, "but I persevered, and one manuscript was finished." She plucked up the courage to send it to a publisher, convinced her book would be rejected. It wasn't, and the rest is history! Penny is married and lives in Cheshire.

## Books by Penny Jordan

### HARLEQUIN PRESENTS

### HARLEQUIN SIGNATURE EDITION

Don't miss any of our special offers. Write to us at the following address for information on our newest releases.

Harlequin Reader Service
901 Fuhrmann Blvd., P.O. Box 1397, Buffalo, NY 14240
Canadian address: P.O. Box 603,
Fort Erie, Ont. L2A 5X3

# PENNY JORDAN

## lovers touch

## *Harlequin Books*

TORONTO • NEW YORK • LONDON
AMSTERDAM • PARIS • SYDNEY • HAMBURG
STOCKHOLM • ATHENS • TOKYO • MILAN

Harlequin Presents first edition November 1989
ISBN 0-373-11216-5

Original hardcover edition published in 1988
by Mills & Boon Limited

Printed in U.S.A.

# CHAPTER ONE

'IS THAT the bride? Where on earth did she get that dress?' Grania demanded disparagingly. 'Honestly, Nell, if Gramps had known what you were going to do with this place when he left it to you, he'd have had forty fits. It's so . . .' she wrinkled her small nose 'so . . .'

'Enterprising?' Nell suggested drily.

They were in the book-room. And the bride whose pretty white dress her stepsister had so disparaged was making her way on the arm of her groom beneath an archway of roses into the marquee that Nell and her small staff had spent the whole of the previous day putting up and organising.

'Enterprising or not, I still say Gramps wouldn't have approved. And you know it.'

That was the trouble. Nell did. Her grandfather had been one of the old school: a stiff, military gentleman, fiercely proud of the tradition of his family and its service to its country. Fiercely loyal to everything he believed in, and that included an old-fashioned and outdated belief that he owed a responsibility, not just to his immediate family, but also to the small village that nestled less than a mile away from Easterhay's front gates.

The village had been there long before the first Hugo de Tressail had built his home there, but it had been under his auspices that the shabby collection of untidy dwellings had been superseded by his manorial hall, and the Norman church with

5

its square tower that overlooked the gentle roll of the Cheshire plain.

In the small church itself, a tomb marked the burial place of that first de Tressail, his stone effigy lying at rest on top of it in the classic medieval pose. Alongside him lay his wife, a small dog curled at her feet.

She had been a Saxon Thane's daughter, well born but poor, and it was supposed to be from her that every now and then throughout the generations a de Tressail woman would inherit her wheat-blonde Saxon hair.

Nell had it herself, a straight waterfall of pale straw which she privately thought colourless. She would much rather have had her stepsister's more vivid colouring, with its inheritance of Latin ancestry.

'I wish I'd known you'd got one of these dos on this weekend,' Grania continued disagreeably. 'I'd never have bothered coming down.'

'Then why did you?' Nell asked her calmly.

At first sight many people dismissed her as timid and withdrawn, but Nell had her own quiet strengths, her own firmly held beliefs and, so some people considered, more than a touch of her grandfather's notorious stubbornness.

'I need an advance on my allowance,' Grania told her curtly. She saw Nell's face and said sharply, 'Oh, for heaven's sake, don't look so po-faced. Joss won't mind . . .'

'Maybe not, but I don't like you taking money from him,' Nell told her stiffly.

'Why ever not? He is our trustee and it is *our* money, although I'll never understand why Gramps insisted on leaving everything tied up so stupidly.

An allowance until I marry . . . then a small lump
sum. I'd rather have the whole lot now, and I've a
good mind to tell Joss as much.'

'No, don't do that.'

Nell spoke more sharply then she had intended.
Outside, the last few remaining guests had gone into
the marquee. She had been rather surprised at the
success of her small venture into commercialism,
although as yet it was true that she had not made
much of a profit, barely enough to pay the wages of
the staff, in fact; but it was a start. A first small step
on the road to independence . . .

She and Grania were so different, and not just in
looks. Grania had the fiery temperament of her
Italian parents, Nell's stepmother and her first
husband, and she also had her careless, insouciant
attitude towards money.

Her success as a model should have made it
possible for her to earn more than enough to live on,
and not need the small allowance Nell's grandfather
had organised for her, but Grania had never seemed
to realise exactly what their financial situation was.
For all her sophistication—and she was
sophisticated, far more so than Nell herself, who was
three years her senior—she had appeared to have no
idea that the allowance she spoke of so glibly came
not from their grandfather's estate, but from Joss
Wycliffe's own pocket.

But, most shamingly of all, Nell knew that if she
were to tell Grania the truth, she would not feel in
the least mortified but would probably make some
mocking quip about Joss being able to afford to pay
her ten times as much as he did . . . which of course
was true.

There had been a time, some months before her

grandfather's death, when Nell had wondered if Joss's constant visits to Easterhay were perhaps because he hoped to make Grania his wife. It had seemed the only explanation for the unlikely relationship which had sprung up between her grandfather and the man who had no compunction at all about saying that he had clawed his way up virtually from the gutter to achieve the multi-millionaire status he now had.

He had moved into the area three years ago, buying a house on the opposite side of the village. Nell had heard the gossip about him before he moved in, but had scarcely expected that her grandfather would make a close friend of him, not for any snobbish reasons, but simply because her grandfather was a very reserved man, with few friends and the kind of sharp tongue that made people view him askance.

And if it hadn't been for that fateful fall, she doubted if Gramps would even have met Joss.

Despite his age, and the handicap of a severe wound incurred during the action that had earned his KBE, her grandfather had always insisted on walking the five-mile perimeter of the parkland every morning after breakfast. The morning he first met Joss, just after the younger man had moved into the village, it had been frosty, and despite Nell's protests Sir Hugo had insisted on going out, taking with him the German pointer that was his favourite companion. He had been seventy-eight then, crusty and irascible; and Nell had loved him desperately. He was virtually the only family she had.

There was Grania, of course, but she and her step-sister had never been close. Grania had been with her mother and Nell's father at the time of the horrific road accident in Italy which had robbed Lucia de Tressail of her life, and reduced Nell's father to a speechless, bedridden form who never regained consciousness. He had survived his father by a matter of days, never knowing that he had inherited the earldom, and died before Nell had taken in the shock of her grandfather's death. Grania had rung from Italy to break the news, saying, 'It's quite convenient in a way. That hospital must have been dreadfully expensive, and it wasn't as though poor Daddy knew anyone, was it?'

Grania had been taken in by the Italian relatives her mother and Nell's father were on their way to visit. Nell had not accompanied them on that trip, primarily because someone had to remain at home with her grandfather. Naturally, when the news came through of her stepmother's death and the full extent of her father's injuries, it had been to her grandfather and Easterhay that she had turned.

Easterhay had been her home for as long as she could remember. Her father, an army man like his father and grandfather before him, had brought her there when she was little more than a few weeks old, leaving her in the care of his father and unmarried aunt.

His wife, Nell's mother, had died at Nell's birth and she had grown up here at Easterhay, unknowing of how out of date her grandfather's mode of life was, because she had never experienced anything else.

She had been five when her father had remarried, but because of his overseas postings Nell had been eight years old before she had ever been able to spend anything more than a brief holiday with her father and new stepmother.

Lucia had tried to be kind to her; she was naturally warm-hearted, Nell recognised; but she, a child reared by a crusty retired general and his maiden sister, had shrunk from Lucia's attempts to embrace and mother her, both literally and metaphorically. A shy, withdrawn child, she had grown up into an equally withdrawn adult, quite happily giving up her job in London to come home and nurse her grandfather when her aunt died, and Gramps announced that she would have to return home to take up her aunt's duties.

She had been just twenty then, and that had been over four years ago. Four years during which she had been forced to mature abruptly, once she realised how precariously balanced her grandfather's finances were.

The care of his son had eaten into his last small reserves of cash, and now with Gramps himself dead and the ominous threat of double death-duties hanging over Easterhay, Nell had no idea how on earth she was going to keep her promise to her grandfather.

Deathbed promises were like something from Dickens, she told herself as she watched her efficient staff close the entrance to the marquee. In a few mintues she would have to go down and preside over the buffet. No matter how much Grania might choose to deride today's bride, her parents had still paid and paid well for their daughter to have her wedding reception here in Easterhay's beautiful parkland, and the pride Nell had inherited from her grandfather, the sense of duty which living with him had instilled in her, would not allow her to do less than her very best for anyone.

'Promise me you will keep Easterhay,' Gramps had demanded almost with his last breath, and she, tears in her eyes and clogging her throat, had agreed.

But she still had no idea how that promise was going to be kept.

Oh, she was doing what she could . . . These weddings brought in a small income, kept the staff busy and paid, and also allowed her to give much needed weekend work to some of the youngsters from the village.

There was also her plan to take in weekend guests, but first some of the bedrooms needed to be renovated. She could hardly expect people to pay to use the one cold and very draughty bathroom installed on both of the two bedroom floors. Deftly she added up her small profit, wondering if she could manage to get three more bathrooms installed by Christmas. She had the workforce to do it . . . Gramps had insisted on keeping on a large staff even though there was little enough for them to do, other than to try to continually repair the fabric of the house as best they could.

Peter Jansen, the estate carpenter, had made the tables for inside the marquee. Harry White, the gardener, had supplied the flowers and helped her make the decorative arrangements. Mrs Booth, the cook/housekeeper, had organised the food, all of them only too glad to be doing something to lift a little of the burden from Nell's shoulders.

Once, they and their children would have found well-paid work in Manchester or Liverpool, but those days were gone. Work wasn't easy to come by anywhere now, and scarcely a week went by without Nell being asked if it was possible for her to find a job for 'our Jane' or 'our Robert' . . .

It was true that the staff lived relatively cheaply and well in the row of cottages owned by the estate, but the cottages were in need of repair, and Nell had no idea how on earth she was going to manage to finance her wages bill once it was winter.

It had occurred to her that she could always hire out the ballroom for private dances, but how many times? This was a very quiet part of Cheshire not favoured by the wealthy, and there was very little demand for such affairs, especially with Chester and the very prestigious Grosvenor Hotel so close.

Weddings were different, and there could be no better setting for a summer wedding than the parkland of Easterhay, with the house itself as a backdrop, sunlight reflecting on the ancient leaded windows set into their stone mullions.

It had been a Jacobean de Tressail who had added the impressive frontage and extra wings to the original house. One wing connected to the stable block, the other via a covered walkway to the orangery, now sadly denuded of its glass and in a state of disrepair.

'I must go out and check on how thing are going . . .'

'Do they pay extra for having the "Lady of the Manor" serve them?' Grania asked her with a sneer. 'They should do.'

Nell lost her temper with her. She had been under a constant strain since her grandfather's death, and although she sympathised with her stepsister, she couldn't stop herself from saying tartly, 'You shouldn't sneer at them, Grania, since it's people like the Dobsons who have the commodity you seem to covet. They're extremely wealthy.'

Compunction swamped her when she saw the way that Grania's eyes filled with tears.

'There's no need for you to be so horrid to me, Nell,' she complained tearfully. 'It's not my fault that I hate being poor. Mama always said that . . .'

She broke off and bit her lip, and Nell guessed that she had been about to say that her mother had always told her that the de Tressail family was a wealthy one.

Sighing faintly, Nell dragged her attention away from the wedding and turned to her stepsister.

'Gramps always liked to pretend that there was more money then there was. His pride wouldn't allow him to admit how bad things were. And then, when Dad died . . . the death-duties . . .' She saw Grania's mutinous face and reflected that, in her way, her stepsister was as stubborn as her grandfather.

'You must have noticed just from the house how bad things are, Grania,' she counselled gently.

'I thought it was just Gramps being mean. You know how he was . . if things are that bad why on earth don't you sell this place? It would fetch a fortune. It's not fair!' she burst out passionately. 'Why should Gramps have left it all to you? It should have been split between us . . .'

Nell stared at her, her heart sinking. She knew these temperamental moods of Grania's of old, and winced mentally at the thought of the fiery outburst to come. Why was it that her stepsister always made her feel like such a pale shadow, a mere reflection when contrasted with her own glowing, brilliant colour?

Her stepsister had so many advantages . . . She was young, beautiful, intelligent . . . She had an excellent career, every advantage, and yet still she resented Nell. And why? Because *she* had inherited Easterhay.

Nell bit down on her bottom lip, gnawing at it,

worrying at it as she tried to find words tactful enough to explain the reasoning behind their grandfather's decision.

Grania and Gramps had never got on. Gramps had never really approved of his son's second marriage, and he had been even less pleased when he'd learned that his second wife already had a child from a previous marriage. Where was the grandson who would inherit the title? Where was the next Sir Hugo? he had demanded when the new bride announced that she didn't want any more children. That had shocked him, Nell knew, and he had never really forgiven Lucia for not providing an heir for Easterhay.

In her grandfather's eyes, Nell knew, Grania was not a de Tressail, and that was one of the reasons he had left Easterhay itself solely to Nell.

Now that title would go to Nell's son . . . always supposing she had one. Always supposing she met a man willing to marry her and shoulder with her the problems of her inheritance.

At heart, she knew that Grania had a valid argument. The property should be sold either as a home to someone rich enough to afford it, or perhaps even to a developer. But Nell knew she would rather have torn out her own heart than agree to such a course of action. Perhaps after all there was more of her grandfather in her than she knew. Or perhaps it was simply conditioning . . . simply the fact that she had been brought up to put Easterhay and all that it stood for before herself and her own needs and desires.

Whatever the case, she knew that her grandfather had left her Easterhay because he saw her as its custodian, that to him she was little more than a trustee holding the house and its lands for the future. But *could* she hold it?

She had no idea . . . but she meant to try.

Trying was one thing, succeeding was another. Her initial approaches to the National Trust on the advice of her solicitor had proved fruitless. If Nell only knew of the houses they were offered, but had to turn down; houses of far more national importance than Easterhay.

The trouble was that Easterhay was too large to be run as home without wealth to support it, and yet too small to be developed in the way that some of the more well known National Trust houses had been.

And so it was down to her to find a means of keeping the estate going, to use what skills she had to bring an income into the bank account, with perilously little in it, to cover the looming death-duties.

She was doing what she could. These weddings that paid so well but demanded so much . . .

Perhaps next year they might even invest in buying their own marquee—that would save money in the long run, and . . .

As always when money worried at her mind, she became totally engrossed in the problems of maintaining the house, and it took Grania's sharp voice to bring her out of her mental financial juggling.

'Well, if *you* won't be reasonable, I'm sure that Joss will . . . He is here, isn't he?'

'If by here you mean in the village, then yes, I believe he is at home at the moment,' Nell acknowledged stiffly.

Grania laughed, her angry mood lightening as she teased, 'Poor Nell, you've never liked him, have you? Far too much the rough diamond for you, I suppose. I must say, though, that he does have a rather exciting aura of sexuality about him. I wonder what he's like in bed.'

'Grania!' Nell protested, her face suddenly hot. It was true that she had always felt uncomfortable in Joss's presence, but not because she didn't like him—far from it!

'Poor Nell,' Grania pouted. 'Honestly, you're like something out of *Pride and Prejudice*. Sex *does* exist, you know. And so does sex appeal, and believe me, Joss has it by the bucketful. All that and money too . . .' She closed her eyes. 'Mmm . . .' She opened them again and looked at her stepsister, saying tauntingly, 'You haven't the foggiest idea what I'm talking about, have you? You wouldn't recognise sex appeal if it . . . Honestly, you're archaic. I suppose you don't even approve of me going to see Joss. You probably even think I should wait for him to get in touch with me. Poor Nell—you've no idea what you're missing.'

Oh, but she had, Nell acknowledged painfully. She was all too well aware of what Grania described as Joss's sexiness . . . She herself would have put it slightly differently, but in essence her stepsister was right. Joss had about him an animal quality of vitality and maleness that no woman could fail to be aware of. And Joss himself knew exactly what he had . . . and he used that knowledge ruthlessly.

He wore the beautiful girls who flocked around him as a hunter wore his trophies. He never seemed to be without some lissom beauty clinging to his arm, and was often photographed on the society pages of the newspapers with some scantily clad female clinging possessively to his dark-suited arm.

Nell often felt that they were deliberately posed,

those photographs, for all their apparent artlessness; the girls were invariably blonde and frail, Joss invariably clothed in the dark formality of a business suit, his face in profile so that the hawklike, almost cruel harshness of his features was thrown into relief.

It was hard to imagine, looking at Joss today, that there had ever been a time when he had been forced to steal to get food . . . when his clothes had been little more than rags.

Now only the faint burr in his voice betrayed him, and even that was a deliberate policy, Nell was sure of it. He was an excellent mimic, and could quite easily have adopted the clipped, classless accent of her grandfather and his kind had he wished. But for some reason he didn't choose to do so; for some reason, as she had good cause to know, he seemed to delight in forcing people to remember the life from which he had sprung.

Nell had once attended a local dinner party with her grandfather when Joss had almost shocked one of the female guests senseless by replying to her polite dinner-table queries about his life by telling her in graphic detail exactly what could happen to small children, both male and female, left to scavenge for a living on the streets of the country's inner cities. He hadn't minced his words and Nell herself had winced, not due to any distaste for the forthrightness of his speech, but for the vivid picture he was drawing.

Unfortunately he had misinterpreted her reaction, and had taunted her for it during the drive home.

It seemed that she and Joss were destined to be at loggerheads with one another, and now if Grania went to him to complain of the unfairness of Gramps' will . . .

Nell could still remember the look on Joss's face when the will was read; the tightening of his mouth that presaged anger; the hard, flat look in his eyes. Odd how well she could recognise every slight nuance of his moods. Or not odd at all, really . . . her stomach quivered and she suppressed the sensation as she had taught herself to suppress every similar sensation and emotion that dwelling on Joss brought.

'Well, I'd better get a move on if I'm going to see Joss . . . I can take your car, can't I?'

'Grania, I'd rather you didn't. I think he's got visitors,' Nell responded stiffly.

'Visitors?' Grania stared at her for a moment, and then burst out laughing.

'You mean one of his women? Oh, he won't mind me interrupting. He's probably bored with her already, knowing Joss.'

'Grania, I'd rather you didn't talk about Joss's private life like that,' Nell interrupted her sharply.

She felt Grania turn to look at her, her stepsister's gaze sharpening.

'I don't believe it,' she said gleefully, after a moment's pause. 'I do believe you've actually fallen for him yourself! Oh, Nell . . . you fool. He'd never look twice at someone like you. He goes for the high-profile glamour types . . .' She eyed Nell's plain skirt and blouse contemptuously. Her stepsister was attractive enough in her own way—she had the most fabulous hair, and her oval face with its wide grey eyes and straight nose had a tranquil beauty which might be out of step with the times, but which was still very appealing.

The trouble with Nell was that she had no idea how to make the most of herself, how to package herself, so to speak. With a modern, voluptuous hair-style, fashionable clothes, heels to give her slim frame height and something fitted to show off her figure, she'd look a million times more appealing . . . but still not appealing enough to entice a man like Joss.

'You'd be much better off with someone like David . . . How is he, by the way?' Grania asked carelessly.

Personally she found the young solicitor who handled their grandfather's business deadly dull, but he would do nicely for Nell, and he would be bound to want to persuade her to get rid of the house. That would suit Grania very well. Once the house was sold, Nell could hardly refuse then to split the proceeds between them. With her share . . . well, the world would be her oyster. She could travel . . . see things . . . do things . . . enjoy the freedom and excitement that she deserved, instead of having to pinch pennies and go cap in hand to Joss for more money.

'Look, I must fly,' Grania announced. 'I've arranged for Terry to pick me up at four. We're having dinner with some friends of his at Aux Quatre Saisons tonight.'

'Terry?' Nell queried.

'You don't know him,' Grania responded brightly. 'I met him at one of the shoots for the underwear commercial. He's in television. By the way,' she added mockingly, 'you do realise, don't you, that what you're doing with the house won't get you into Joss's good books? He doesn't approve at all . . .'

Grania's taunt and its implied hint that she, Grania, was far more *au fait* with Joss's opinions than her dull, boring elder sister, set a spark to the

over-dry tinders of Nell's temper. She had borne so
much these last eight months; struggled so hard to
keep her promise to Gramps; carried the dual
burden of its responsibility and that of knowing their
true financial position, which she was sure Grania
did not. The allowance she talked about so glibly for
instance . . . the money she believed Gramps had left
her. That came from Joss, and it galled Nell more
than anything else on earth that she was forced to
keep silent, to accept his charity.

As her grandfather's executor, he was well aware
of the exact state of their finances, and probably had
been beforehand.

It was odd in a way how much her grandfather
had confided in him . . . how in those last few
months, when it became apparent that he had not
long to live, he had drawn strength from Joss's
presence . . . had even come to rely on him in a way
that he had never relied on her. But to Gramps she
was just a woman—a frail creature who need
protecting and directing.

Joss was different. Joss was a man. During those
last months he had called regularly two and sometimes three times a week, making time in what Nell
knew must be a hectic schedule to come and play
chess with her grandfather in the old-fashioned
panelled library. Yes, there was very little about the
de Tressail finances and the de Tressail family that
Joss didn't know.

Only the week before his death, still chuckling
over some reminiscence of when Joss had described
his roving teenage years when he had falsified his
age and travelled the world working on the huge oil
tankers, Gramps had claimed, 'He's cut out of the
same cloth as the first Sir Hugo, is Joss. A man who

makes his own rules. A bit of a rogue perhaps, but tough enough to hold on to what he considers to be his own. Strong enough to stick by what he believes in. I like him,' he had added staring fiercely up at Nell, as though half expecting her to argue with him.

Now Grania's taunt about Joss's views on what she was trying to do to bring money into the estate infuriated her, and she responded fiercely, 'Well, then, that's just his tough luck, isn't it? Easterhay belongs to me, and what I choose to do or not do with it is *my* business and no one else's, especially not someone like Joss Wycliffe,' she added with far more scorn in her voice then she really felt. The scorn in actual fact was for herself, for feeling hurt by Grania's revelation that she and Joss had discussed her and Joss had revealed his disapproval. Although why she should feel so hurt, so let down . . .

'Unfortunately, that's not strictly true.'

The dry, controlled male voice shocked her, making her spin round, her hand going to her throat in an age-old gesture of self-protection.

'Joss . . . I didn't hear you come in,' she said weakly, knowing that she was flushing to the roots of her pale hair . . . knowing the contrast she must make to Grania's vivid dark beauty, Grania who had no hesitation at all in running lightly across the room and flinging herself into Joss's arms.

Only she didn't quite make it. He fielded her off very neatly just before she reached him, holding her at arm's length while she pouted and eyed him with wicked flirtatiousness.

Oh, to be Grania and not her dull, boring self!

'Joss, the very person!' Grania exclaimed. 'I need to talk to you desperately. How on earth did you know I was here?'

'I didn't,' Joss told her flatly. 'I came to see Nell . . .'

'Oh, well, that can wait. Besides, Nell's just about to go and do her boring duty by the wedding party. Honestly Joss, you ought to see the fright of a dress the bride's wearing. Home-made, I'm sure . . .' Chattering blithely, linking her arm through Joss's she led him out of the room.

Nell watched them, her face shadowed with pain. What a striking couple they made, both so tall and dark. Joss lithely male in his casual clothes, the leather blouson jacket he was wearing so soft that it promised to feel like purest silk to the touch; Grania, dressed in something wildly fashionable and no doubt wildly expensive, while she . . .

She looked down at her serviceable tweed skirt and blouse. They were good-quality separates, but she had had them for about six years, and they had not been bought for fashion's sake then. What on earth had prompted her to choose beige in the first place? Her aunt, of course. Aunt Honoria had strong views on the dress and manners of young women. Nell had been eighteen when those clothes had been bought. Just leaving college and starting her first job at the small publishers' run by an old friend of her grandfather, and the clothes had been those Aunt Honoria had deemed most suitable for her business life.

Like everything else in her wardrobe, they had simply become things to put on so that she could get on with the business of living . . . dull and worthy, like herself.

The sound of Grania's excited laughter floated back towards her. In the dimness of the corridor, she could just see how Joss's dark head inclined slightly toward her stepsister's, and a pain she knew she ought to have learned to control three years ago knifed through her.

Joss Wycliffe . . . the very last man on earth she ought to fall in love with. And yet she had . . . instantly . . . on sight . . . and without any chance of ever recovering from the blow that fate had dealt her.

It was just three years ago that she had first met Joss, and she would never forget that heart-stopping moment when she had come to the door in answer to its imperative summons and discovered Joss standing outside supporting her grandfather, who had fallen over and hurt himself while out for his walk.

Joss had been wearing brief running shorts and a singlet, his dark hair sweat—slick, but still inclined to curl slightly. He had been tanned, his skin like Grania's, naturally far darker than her own.

The sight of him had totally overwhelmed her, and she had behaved, she suspected, like an idiot, staring at him as though she had never seen a man in her life before. Who knew what foolish dreams she might have started weaving in her head if Joss hadn't looked at her and said coolly, 'Yes. Shockingly disreputable, aren't I, and hardly dressed to make the acquaintance of a *lady?*' And he had stressed that last word unmercifully, making her colour up painfully.

And she had seen in his eyes his contempt and dismissal of her; had seen how totally unattractive as a woman he found her, and for the first time in her life she had truly appreciated her Aunt Honoria's training. As she had gone on appreciating it ever since. If nothing else, it enabled her to act out the role life had designed for her: the unmarried, unattractive daughter of the house who knew her place; and to conceal from Joss exactly what effect he had on her, or so she hoped . . .

# CHAPTER TWO

BY TUESDAY the wedding marquee had been taken down, the tables and chairs packed away and the lawn restored to its normal pristine splendour.

Nell was sitting in the library, working on her accounts. She kept these meticulously, amused to discover that she had quite a talent for book-keeping; but unfortunately, like all her other talents, it wasn't enough to build a career on—at least, not the kind of career that would support a house like Easterhay. For that, one needed a business empire to rival Joss's.

She looked again at her neat figures, her heart sinking. It didn't matter how many corners she tried to cut, how many economies she made, she just wasn't making enough money. Last weekend's wedding had been the next to the last of the season. So far she had managed to keep on all the staff, but with winter approaching . . .

Her grandfather's pension had died with him, and although Joss might have come to some arrangement with her grandfather to ensure that Grania had her allowance, Nell was damned if she was going to allow him to support her as well.

Outside, her car sparkled in the autumn sunshine. She ought to drive into Chester to collect some supplies. Her car was only two years old, an expensive model that she would never have dreamed of buying, but which her grandfather had insisted on giving her as a birthday present. Each time she looked at it, she mentally calculated how much she could get for it, but how could she sell Gramps' last gift to her . . . a gift she was sure he could barely afford himself?

He had excused his generosity, saying testily that, since he was no longer allowed to drive, she would have to act as his chauffeur, and that he was damned if he was going to be driven about the place in one of those poky modern things.

But a Daimler . . . for someone in her financial position? She leaned back in the leather chair which had once been her grandfather's. It was too large for her, and not very comfortable.

She closed her eyes tiredly, only to open them again in shock as she heard Joss saying tauntingly, 'Finding the old man's chair too big for you, Nell? Just like his shoes, eh?'

'Joss! What are you doing here?'

She sat up, flustered that he should have caught her off guard. She was already all too well aware of the most comical contrast she must be to the women in his life . . . beautiful, expensively groomed women. She hated him seeing her when she wasn't prepared.

'It's quarter day—remember?'

Quarter day . . . of course Her grandfather still had stuck by the old-fashioned calendar all his life, and he had left intructions in his will that every quarter day she was to present her household accounts to Joss, as first his wife and then his sister had once presented theirs to him.

'Oh, yes, the accounts. Well, they're all here.'

She got up tiredly, so that he could take her seat and study the books open in front of her. As she stood, her body reacted to its tiredness and she stumbled awkwardly, catching her hipbone on the corner of the desk. The impact sent a shock-wave of pain through her, making her catch her bottom lip between her teeth.

She saw Joss frown, the amber eyes flaming as they always did when he was annoyed. Of course, her clumsiness would be offensive to a man used to women who only moved with elegance.

'You look as though you haven't slept in a month, and you're too thin,' he told her brutally. 'What the hell are you doing to yourself?'

'Nothing,' Nell countered, adding pettishly for some reason she couldn't define, 'I wish you wouldn't allow Grania to believe that her allowance comes from Gramps' estate, Joss. It makes it difficult for me.'

'You know she believes this place should be sold and the proceeds split between you?' he interrupted her.

Nell gripped the edge of the desk with slender fingers and agreed bleakly. 'Yes.'

'But of course your grandfather felt, as she isn't a de Tressail by birth, that she should be excluded from inheriting from the estate. A court of law might very probably take a different point of view.'

Nell swallowed painfully. Was Joss telling her that he shared Grania's view that Gramps had been unfair in not leaving the house to them jointly?

'Gramps wanted the house to stay with the family. He hated the thought of it being sold.'

She had to blink back emotional tears and keep her face averted from him. She wasn't like Grania, she couldn't cry prettily. At Gramps' funeral she had been too anguished to do anything more than simply watch in frozen silence. It had been Grania who wept, silent, pretty tears that barely touched her make-up; her head restling vulnerably against Joss's chest.

She had watched them, telling herself she was a fool for the jealousy she felt. Joss would never look at her. In the three years she had known him, the only time he had come anywhere near embracing her had been the first Christmas. He had arrived at the house on Christmas Eve to see her grandfather. Nell had let him in and his eyes had gone briefly to the mistletoe hanging in the hall, and then to her mouth as he stepped inside. Even now she could still feel her pulses flutter dangerously at the recollection of that moment when she had known he was going to kiss her.

His mouth had been hard and warm and she had quivered in his arms, unable to hold back the sensations storming her. He had released her immediately, stepping back from her, and she was sure she had read derision in his eyes as her grandfather came into the hall to welcome him.

He had not touched her since, and she could hardly blame him. She was not his type of woman and she never would be.

'I know,' Joss told her drily. 'One could almost say, in fact, that he was obsessed with it, to the point where the continuation of the de Tressail name and the family's occupation of this house were more important to him than anything else. More important than you, for instance, Nell,' he added cruelly.

'Yes . . . he never really got over the fact that my father had no son,' she agreed evenly, ignoring the look in his eyes.

'Do you know what his plans were, had he remained alive?' Joss asked her abruptly.

Nell looked at him. 'Plans for what?'

'For the continuation of the de Tressail family,' Joss told her mockingly. 'For your marriage, Nell, and the production of a great-grandson to carry on the name.'

'He had no plans,' Nell told him huskily, frowning as she saw the derision in his eyes. 'Joss, the days are gone when families arranged marriages.'

'Are they? Your grandfather was a desperate man, and desperate men do strange things. Six months before he died, your grandfather asked me if I would marry you.'

Nell was stunned, her white face giving away her feelings.

'Surprised, Nell, that he should even consider such a marriage? With a self-made man like myself with no breeding or background; no family history stretching back for generation upon generation? But you forget one thing. I have one valuable asset: I'm rich . . . very rich. I have the money that Easterhay so desperately needs.'

Nell wasn't listening. She swung round, her face in her hands as she murmured frantically, 'How could he? Oh, how could he?'

'Quite easily,' Joss told her calmly. 'To him, it was an almost ideal solution to your family's problems.'

Beneath the weight of her shame and betrayal that her grandfather should humiliate her in such a way, she was desperately aware of how amused and contemptuous Joss must be. She was the very last woman he would want as his wife, and no doubt he was now going to enjoy letting her know it.

To stop him she said frantically, 'The whole thing's absurd. Poor Gramps. He was so ill towards the end that . . .'

'His mind was as sound as yours or mine,' Joss interrupted brutally, 'and you know it. What's wrong, Nell? Having second thoughts now that you're actually being called upon to make the ultimate sacrifice? It was all all right when you were playing at being the struggling Lady of the Manor, proudly trying to keep things going, but when a real solution to your problems presents itself, you flinch from taking it. No need to ask myself why, of course. I've no doubt that given your choice, you'd much rather have someone like Williams as a husband.

'Unfortunately though, my dear, *he* has even less money than you do yourself, and you'd never keep this place going with what he earns as a country solicitor. Make your mind up to it, Nell. It's either marry me or sell up.'

'*Marry* you?' Nell stared at him, her eyes dark with shock. 'Joss, you can't possibly be serious about this.'

'Why not?'

'But why? Why would you want to marry me?' She missed the look he gave her.

'How very modest you are,' he said silkily after he had controlled it. 'Surely it's obvious, Nell? I'm a self-made man who's made it financially in life, but, like all self-made men, I now want to crown my financial success with social acceptance. Not just for me, but for my children, especially my sons . . . my eldest son,' he added meaningfully.

And then, in case she hadn't understood, he added coolly, 'Marriage to you will open doors which would otherwise have remained closed. Our son will inherit your grandfather's title . . . Surely, Nell, you know how much men of my class yearn to become members of the aristocracy?'

She was sure he was mocking her. In all the three years she had known him, Joss had never once exhibited the slightest degree of envy for her grandfather's social standing, and it stunned her to discover now that he was actually contemplating marrying her for the reasons he had just stated.

It was her grandfather's fault, of course. He was the one who had initially put the idea in his head, but Joss had obviously not been slow to pick it up.

Unless, of course, he was simply making fun of her, constructing a hugely elaborate joke at her expense. Her common sense told her this was hardly likely.

'Joss, I can't marry you,' she protested, struggling to deny the emotions churning inside her. Our son . . our son . . . the words seemed to reverberate inside her head, until she couldn't hear anything else. In those two words, he had conjured up such an enormity of complex emotions and sensations within her that she could barely accommodate them all. To have a child by this man whom she loved so desperately. To live with him here in this house. To be his wife . . . but she was allowing herself to be swept away into a fantasy world.

Joss wasn't talking about marriage as she envisaged it; he was talking about a coldly calculated business arrangement; a marriage that would have no emotions, no feelings, no love, and that would be nothing other than a mere exchange of assets. His money for her title and home.

It happened, of course it happened, even in these enlightened times, but not to her . . . never to her.

'It was what your grandfather wanted, Nell,' he warned her. 'An ideal solution to a problem which never ceased to worry him.'

How dared he add to her guilt? He knew what he was doing to her by telling her that, although she didn't doubt for a moment that he was telling the truth and that her grandfather had seen it as an ideal solution to their financial problems.

'I can't,' she whispered painfully.

'No . . .? Then I'm afraid you leave me no choice. As Grania's trustee, I really have no alternative but to support her claim to half of your grandfather's estate. In the courts, if necessary. Of course, if we were married, I've no doubt I could come to some suitable arrangement with Grania . . . a lump sum in lieu of what she considers due to her . . .'

Nell stared at him in disbelief and then whispered frozenly, 'That's blackmail.'

The dark eyebrows rose, and her mouth trembled as much with anguish as with anything else.

'These days we call it gamesmanship . . . the art of being one step ahead of your rival.' He flicked back the cuff of the jacket he was wearing. 'I've got to be back in London this evening, and I shan't be back until the early hours. I'll come over in the morning, Nell. You can give me your answer then,' he told her, ignoring her protest that he already had it.

He had no mercy . . . no mercy at all, Nell acknowledged half an hour later. She was huddled over the empty fire, her grandfather's dog at her knee.

The pointer had been a birthday gift from Joss to Gramps, and with the loyalty of her breed had attached herself to him devotedly. She had pined after his death, and although Nell walked her and fed her she came way down the list in the pointer's affections. She was a man's dog, and never failed to place herself at Joss's feet whenever he came to visit. It was unusual for her to show such affection to Nell, but today, sensing her despair, she had come to sit beside her and Nell welcomed the warmth of her body, hugging her in her arms as she rocked slowly to and fro, trying to come to terms with Joss's proposal.

Even now she could hardly take it in. Joss wanted to marry her, and how brutally he had made sure that she was not likely to harbour any illusions about the reasons behind his proposal.

He didn't want *her* . . . No, what he wanted was her home . . . her name . . . her family title . . . for his son . . . their son . . . And he had made no apology for wanting them either; but then, why should he? To Joss, everything in life was a commodity with a price on it. The price of the gift he wanted to give his son was marriage to her. It was as simple as that.

The phone rang abruptly, making her jump. It was the vicar's wife, reminding her that she was bringing the Young Wives up to the house to tour round the greenhouses later in the week.

If only there was someone she could turn to for advice and counsel. Her closest friend throughout her schooldays was now married, with a busy household, her husband being a doctor. They lived near Cambridge, and as well as her own baby girl there were also two older children from Robert's first marriage. It hadn't been easy for her friend to make the decision to take on a widower with two young children, and there had been many long telephone calls between Liz and Nell before Liz had finally decided to commit herself to Robert.

Now she was blissfully happy, and fully deserved to be, and yet for all the confidences they had shared over the years, Nell had never told her how she felt about Joss. Perhaps she had hoped that by keeping silent she could somehow pretend that those feelings didn't exist?

But they did, and today Joss had scoured her soul by what he had said to her; by the ruthlessness he had displayed; by his total lack of any consideration of her own feelings.

How could she possibly marry him? And yet, how could she not . . .? She had promised Gramps that she would do everything in her power to hold on to Easterhay; how could she live with herself if she refused to honour that promise?

It was easy to tell herself that her grandfather was the product of a different age, that her promise need not be kept . . . that no one would blame her for refusing Joss, bearing in mind his reasons for marrying her. It should be the easiest thing in the world for her to simply say 'No', but she couldn't. Conscience . . . pride . . . or just sheer, stubborn love for her home and her family . . . She didn't really know which, or if it was a combination of all three. Or even perhaps if she had inherited more from her reckless ancestress then just her blonde hair, and, for the first time in her life, was actually going to throw herself blindly into the arms of fate.

The morning papers brought in the shocking realisation that Joss wasn't leaving anything to chance. There was a photograph of him prominently displayed on the society page of *The Times*, and underneath the caption, 'Millionaire entrepreneur Joss Wycliffe announces that he is shortly to be married. The bride is not Naomi Charters, the actress whom he has currently been escorting, but the daughter of an old friend, Lady Eleanor de Tressail. The couple will marry within the next few months.'

Nell sat down at the breakfast-table, feeling faintly sick. How dared Joss take her acceptance for granted like this! He wasn't allowing her anything . . . no pride, no compassion . . . nothing.

She pushed away her bowl of cereal and reached for the coffee-pot, her hand trembling.

There was a large pile of mail beside her plate, and it contained far too many ominous buff envelopes. She picked up the top one, her heart sinking as she recognised the familiar Inland Revenue stamp. When she opened it her heart sank even further.

It was a reminder that there were still death-duties to be paid, and the sum seemed astronomical. On the other side of the panelled dining-room was a lighter piece of panelling where a Gainsborough had once hung. It had been sold when her grandmother died. Now there was nothing more to sell . . . Other than herself . . . She shivered tensely. Dear God, why on earth couldn't Joss have at least tried to make it easy for her . . . at least pretended to feel something for her, even if they both knew it *was* a pretence? This way . . . this way . . . he was making sure that she knew exactly what it was he wanted out of their marriage, and it wasn't her.

The phone rang, and she knew before she picked it up that it would be Joss.

She was right; his clipped, slightly accented voice was abrasive on her ear.

'I'm coming over at twelve, and I've arranged for Williams to be there at one. There'll be certain legal

arrangements to be made and I thought you'd want
him there, seeing as he's your solicitor . . .'

He was moving too fast. Bullying her . . . pushing
her in a direction she wasn't sure she wanted to go;
but when she tried to protest he hung up on her. She
could picture him without even trying. He would be
standing in his study, an anonymous square room,
which like the rest of his house looked more like an
expensive hotel than a home.

He would probably be wearing one of those fine
Savile Row wool suits in some dark, formal fabric.
Joss liked good clothes and he wore them well, but
nothing could totally disguise what her grandfather
had described as his buccaneering quality; that
arrogant maleness that no amount of city suiting
could tame.

His dark hair would be lying flat to his skull, thick
and clean, his mouth curled into that thin, taunting
smile he gave her so often; nothing like the smile he
gave other women.

She got up unsteadily and called to the dog,
Heicker. She came to heel obediently. Joss had
trained her.

Outside it was one of those crisp September days
when frost and the scent of woodsmoke mingled in
the air and the sky was a clear pale blue with the sun
dappling yellow and bright through the turning
leaves.

Deliberately Nell avoided walking past the greenhouses and the stables which had once housed her
grandfather's hunters. She herself liked to ride, but
she did not enjoy hunting other than for its
pageantry. She was too squeamish, too conscious of
the purpose for which the hounds were bred, and as
a teenager she had always drawn a sigh of relief

when the day ended without the fox being caught.

Her grandfather had had no such qualms, of course. To him, fox were vermin and hunting a sport. Right up until his death, the local hunt had started their Boxing Day meet at Easterhay. The traditional stirrup cup prepared in the kitchen for the huntsmen came from a recipe supposedly brought back from France by a de Tressail who had been exiled there by Henry VII and whose French wife was supposed to have been connected to the powerful de Guise family, uncles of Mary Stuart through her French mother. Whatever its true origins, it went down well with the huntsmen. She wondered if Joss would want to continue the tradition. Did he hunt? she wondered. Certainly not from birth as her father and grandfather had done, but at some point or other in his life Joss had taken enough time away from making money to acquire a sophisticated degree of polish.

Despite Joss's taunts, Nell was no snob. Although he didn't seem to realise it, she admired Joss for what he had achieved, and her doubts about the wisdom of marrying him had nothing to do with the fact that he had been born in a Glaswegian slum and she in an expensive private nursing home.

Twelve o'clock, he had said . . . it was gone ten now. And then David arriving at one . . . He was determined to make her agree, then. Even to the extent of involving the family solicitor. Poor David, how little he understood the Josses of this world. Nell suspected that David was terrified of Joss, although he hid it beneath a stiffly formal manner more suited to a man of fifty-odd than one of twenty-six.

Like her, David had been brought up in an old-

fashioned tradition, knowing almost from the cradle
that he was destined to succeed his father as a
country solicitor. There had been a time when she
had wondered if she might fall in love with him. But
that had been before she saw Joss.

For some reason she couldn't entirely analyse
herself, she chose to wait for him, not in her
grandfather's library, the room with which she was
most familiar in the house, but in a small, north-
facing sitting-room which three centuries before had
been the preserve of the ladies of the family, and
which was now never used, as testified to by the fine
film of dust on the small French escritoire. She
touched it idly, admiring the delicate marquetry
work. This desk had been part of the dowry of the
family's second French bride, Louise, a shy, prim-
looking child of fourteen who had died giving birth
to her first child, and whose portrait hung next to
that of her husband in the long gallery.

The air in the room was faintly musty. A distinct
chill penetrated through Nell's thin blouse, and
when she saw Joss drive up she shivered violently,
hugging her arms around her body.

He wasn't in his Rolls, but driving the Aston
Martin. Its rich plum paintwork went well with his
dark colouring, she noted idly, as after swinging
long legs from the car, he straightened up and closed
the door.

Even the way he moved had a certain animal
assurance; no hesitation or doubts there, Nell
reflected wryly as he walked towards the main
entrance looking neither to his left nor his right, his
head not downbent as so many people's were when
they walked, but tilted at an arrogant angle.

Anyone not knowing him would think he was

more at home here in this house than herself, Nell
acknowledged.

Her grandfather's staff were old-fashioned and set
in their ways, and she knew that Johnson, who had
been her grandfather's batman and then his valet,
and who was now supposed to be retired, but who
had begged her to allow him to stay on at the house,
rather than retire to the estate cottage her grandfather had left him, would insist on announcing Joss
formally to her before allowing him admittance to
the room.

Against one wall of the small room, painted to
pick out the soft colours of the faded blue silk
wallpaper, was a small table decorated with gilded
flowers, and above it a matching mirror.

It gave Nell back her reflection with the cruel
honesty of the room's northern light. Not plain
precisely, but certainly not lushly beautiful like the
women she had seen photographed with Joss. Her
features were neat and regular, surprisingly dark
lashes surrounding the clear grey of her eyes, her
skin, that delicate, translucent, very English skin
that looked its best under softly rainwashed skies.

All her life, almost, she had worn her hair plaited,
and the neatly twisted coils lying flat against her
skull heightened the delicacy of her bone-structure,
but Nell saw none of the rare delicacy of her
features, seeing instead only that she was a pale,
washed-out shadow of her stepsister's dark beauty.

As a teenager she had experimented with make-
up, trying to copy the effects she had seen in
magazines, but on her the effects had been garish,
and so now she rarely wore more than pale pink
lipstick.

Liz had tried to persuade her into Harvey Nichols

the Christmas before last when they had met in
London for a shopping trip, telling her that modern
make-ups with their subtle colours were far more
suited to her delicate colouring than those which had
been fashionable during their early teens, but, all too
aware of the fact that Grania was coming home for
Christmas, Nell had shrunk from inviting Joss's
mockery by doing anything that might be construed as
an attempt to catch his attention.

The salon door opened and Joss walked in, making
her step back from the mirror.

'Where's Johnson?' she asked him huskily, flustered
to see him standing there when she had anticipated a
few more moments' grace.

Something gleamed in Joss's eyes, something
predatory and intimidating, but when he spoke his
voice was cool and distant.

'Since I'm shortly to become a member of the
family, I told him there was no need to stand on
ceremony.'

Nell gripped the edge of the table.

'You told Johnson that we're going to be
married?'

'You object? Why? We *are* going to be married,
aren't we, Nell?'

She looked mutely at him and then said sadly, 'Do
I have any choice?'

'No—and I haven't said a word to Johnson,' he
told her calmly. 'I'm not totally without awareness,
Nell . . . *some* of the rough edges have been rubbed
off, you know. I know you will want to tell the staff
our good news yourself . . .'

There was an ironic look in his eyes as he said the
words 'our good news' and, despite her firm
determination not to do so, Nell felt herself flushing . . .

although surely there was nothing for her to feel guilty about. *Joss* was the one who had proposed their marriage. Joss was the supplicator, no matter how hard she found it to visualise him in that role. When she gave him her answer . . . And then she realised that she already had. Her lips parted on an uncertain breath, and, as though he read her mind, Joss said mockingly, 'Too late, you've already committed yourself, Nell. Besides——'

He broke off as there was a discreet tap on the door and the housekeeper came in carrying a tray of coffee.

'Thank you, Mrs Booth.' Joss reached out and took the tray, giving the older woman a far warmer smile than Nell had ever received from him, making a faint flush of colour rise up under her plump cheeks as she left.

'I didn't ask for any coffee,' Nell told him once they were alone.

She had been astounded by the way he already seemed to have taken control . . . by the way the staff, *her* staff, were already responding to him.

'No? Just as well I did, then. When Johnson told me you were waiting for me in here, I thought we'd need it. As I remembered it, this room gets as cold as charity . . . No doubt that was why it was chosen by the French martyr . . .'

He looked amused at the astonishment on her face.

'Did you really think me totally ignorant of the family's history, Nell? Your grandfather told it to me . . . I am right, aren't I? This sitting-room was furnished by Louise de Roget, wasn't it?'

'Yes,' Nell told him bleakly.

'Poor, unhappy little French child. I believe she

spent more time at her prayers than in her husband's bed. Our marriage won't be like that, Nell.'

She looked up at him, shocked by the note of steel certainty in his voice.

'I know you want a son, Joss,' she told him with dignity.

'More than one,' he told her frankly. 'And not just sons . . . I want a family, Nell.'

'And if I don't?' she returned with spirit, but he ignored her challenge, smiling that cruel smile, and taking her chin between his thumb and forefinger so that she was forced to look directly at him.

'Ah, but you do,' he told her softly. 'You were made for motherhood, Nell, and if you're thinking of Williams as the father of your children, then forget him.'

'David? But . . .'

'Your grandfather seemed to think you might be fancying yourself in love with him—forget him. Nell, he might be able to afford you, but he can't afford this house.'

What he said was in essence true, but that didn't make it any the less insulting, not just to herself but to David as well.

To cover up the tremor in her stomach, she said sharply, 'That remark is chauvinistic in the extreme.'

But Joss only laughed. 'Give in, Nell. Admit that marriage to me will solve all your problems. No more closed-off cold rooms . . . No more pinching and scraping . . . No more nights lying awake, worrying about how you're going to cope . . .'

How little he knew . . . Now her sleepless nights would be spent worrying about about how she was going to cope with loving him, living with him and trying to hide how she felt.

'There's another thing,' he said as he released her chin and she jerked her head away.

As far as he was concerned, it was settled—they were to be married; and yet he had made not the slightest attempt to touch her . . . to embrace her . . . to make her feel that he felt something for her other than a mere desire to use her.

'You're going to need to buy yourself some new clothes. I'll organise a credit card for you so that the bills can be sent direct to me. Fiona, my secretary, will help you. You'll probably need to arrange to spend a couple of days in London. I'll get her to organise something.'

Nell was furious. She had heard the gossip in the village about the relationship which was supposed to exist between Joss and the elegant woman who worked for him, commuting each day from her home in Chester to Joss's house. But, even more than his assumption that she was not capable of choosing her own clothes, she resented the contemptuous glance he had given the outfit she was wearing, no matter how much it might merit it. With that single look he had made it more than clear how very unattractive he found her.

'Thank you,' she told him arctically, 'but I really don't need any new clothes, Joss. I already possess a perfectly adequate wardrobe.'

'Yes,' he agreed drily, 'and I'm sure it's as antiquated as its contents. What's the matter with you, Nell?' he demanded, rounding on her. 'What possible pleasure can it give you to dress like a retired schoolteacher? Tweed skirts . . . twin sets. Wake up, Nell; not even the Royal family dress like that these days.'

It struck her as she listened to him that he was probably ashamed of her; embarrassed about how she would look in comparison with the women he normally favoured; worried that the outside world might take one look at her and know immediately why he had married her; and that hurt.

'I'm sorry if my present appearance doesn't please you, Joss,' she told him when she had control of herself. 'What a pity you can't simply wave a magic wand and transform me, without all this tiresome fuss.'

She saw that he was about to say something and hurried on bitterly, 'Of course, one other alternative would be to simply allow me to fade into the background of your life. After all, I can imagine how awkward it will be for you . . . Joss Wycliffe having a plain, dull wife . . .'

'Oh, no, you don't, Nell,' he interrupted her harshly. 'I'm not having you sneaking off with Williams behind my back. I want a wife who is going to play her full role in my life, in public and in private.'

Nell looked at him, astonished that he could actually think she was romantically interested in David, but forbearing to say anything. Let him think what he liked, she decided rebelliously, still deeply resentful of his insults about her clothes, even if she knew at heart that they were justified.

'No need to look so tragic. I thought you'd be more sensible than this Nell. Your grandfather was almost proud when he pointed out to me the rich brides brought into the family through arranged marriage. Even down to the mill-owner's daughter whose father's millions came into the family after

Waterloo. Pity her son turned out to be such a gambler and lost the lot. If he hadn't . . .'

She lifted pain-blinded eyes to his face, desperately seeking some softness there, some glimmer of compassion, but there was none. She meant nothing to him, other than a means to an end, and she never would; she would die before she allowed him to guess how much she loved him.

She saw him glance at his watch. 'I have to leave immediately after we've seen Williams, and there are several things we still have to sort out. The staff . . . As far as I'm concerned you are free to make whatever arrangements you choose, but Audlem, my chauffeur, will come with me, and I'd like you to make sure that there's always a spare bedroom ready for Fiona. As you know, I prefer to work from home when I can. I suspect that the only place we're going to be able to install my computer equipment is in one of the cellars. I'll get someone round to check on that . . . I want it in before we get married. How much time will you need? I thought a month. That will give Williams time to draw up the agreements . . .'

He saw her face and smiled mirthlessly. 'We may as well do this properly, Nell. I'll make you a monthly allowance, for yourself, and open another account for you to run the house from. You're going to find yourself very busy over the next few months with interior designers and the like. I want this place completely refurbished.'

'All of it?' Nell demanded faintly.

'All of it,' he confirmed. 'So, Nell, can you be ready in a month? We'll have the wedding breakfast here, of course. I'l give you a list of the people I want inviting. Fiona will help you with the invites, etc.'

'Joss . . . Surely a quiet wedding . . .'

'As though we've something to hide? I think not.'

He broke off as David Williams drove up.

This time Johnson did announce the visitor, and David came in, looking slightly flustered and concerned.

'Nell!' he exclaimed, going towards her, and Nell suspected he would have kissed her if Joss hadn't suddenly placed himself between them and said forcefully,

'You can congratulate me, Williams. Nell has agreed to become my wife . . .'

For a moment David looked too shocked to speak, and when he did it was to Nell, not to Joss.

'Is this true, Nell?'

'Yes,' she told him quietly.

Out of the corner of her eye she saw Joss watching them narrowly and then tranferring his attention to his watch, a slim, gold masculine timepiece. Odd, in someone so devoted to modern technology, that he should choose a very traditional kind of watch; traditional and expensive, but discreetly so; not for Joss the status symbol of the 'in' designer watch, she reflected acidly.

'We've a lot to discuss, Williams,' Joss announced, coming between them. The shock of his hand resting proprietorially on her arm made Nell flinch in surprise and then wince as she felt his fingers bite warningly into her flesh before he released her. She was trembling, slightly horrified at how very vulnerable she was to him physically.

David looked dazed when Joss had finished telling him exactly what was happening.

Nell felt equally dazed as she heard him name what seemed like an impossible sum, adding carelessly that he was giving it to her as a marriage settlement.

'And I take it that Nell will be free to take it with her, should the marriage ever come to an end,' David said stiffly.

Instantly Nell saw the golden eyes flash dangerously.

'Only death will end our marriage,' she heard Joss telling him.

She knew why, of course, and she suspected that David shared her knowledge, because when Joss had finished dictating to him the terms of the various agreements, he burst out explosively, 'Nell, are you sure you know what you're doing? Do you really intend to marry him?'

'Yes,' she told him quietly. There could be no going back. She was committed. David looked at her unhappily and then turned angrily to Joss, only to hesitate as Joss studied him, one eyebrow lifted in mocking interrogation.

'You seem surprised?'

'Not that you want to marry Nell,' David muttered, flushed and obviously resentful, 'but I can't see why Nell would want to marry you. I realise exactly what *you'll* get out of this marriage. But what about Nell? What does she get out of it?'

There was a tiny pause, and then Joss looked directly at her, his eyes hard and brilliant.

'Oh, Nell will get me,' he said in a very soft voice.

Her heart almost stopped. He had *known* all the time . . . He had just been playing with her, a cruel, vicious kind of torment, when all along he had *known* how vulnerable she was, how unable to refuse him anything . . . even though it meant sacrificing her pride and her self-respect.

'And, of course, my money,' he continued, his voice less soft and very cynical, and relief flowed through her as she realised he had not guessed how she felt at all.

David left just after two. Nell watched him walk to his car, his shoulders hunched defensively. He paused and looked up at the window.

Nell hadn't realised Joss was standing so close to her and she stiffened in shock as she felt his hands on her shoulders, drawing her back against his body, one hand holding her imprisoned while the other lifted to her throat, caressing the tender flesh as though he were actually her lover.

When she felt his mouth against the other side of her throat she cried out softly and then started to tremble violently.

No one had kissed her like this before, caressing the sensitive hollows with knowing expertise, making her shiver and tense beneath the ripples of sensation that ricocheted through her body.

In a daze she saw David stare at them, white-faced, and then get into his car. Behind her she could feel the hard muscles of Joss's body, and when she tried to pull away, his fingers bit painfully into her collarbone.

It was only when David had gone that he released her.

'Why did you do that?' she stormed furiously, her face burning hot flags of colour.

'Why do you think?' Joss retorted. 'You're going to be *my* wife, Nell.'

'You didn't do it because of that. You did it because David was watching us.'

'Exactly,' Joss agreed curtly. 'As I just said, you're going to be *my* wife.' He smiled thinly as he

watched her. 'Such delicate skin.' He lifted his hand
and, thinking he meant to touch her again, Nell
flinched back, only to feel a resurgence of heat burn
her face as he simply looked at his watch and then
said curtly, 'There'll be formal announcements to be
sent to the papers . . . but Fiona will see to that.'

Nell saw the look he gave her and her face burned.
Without saying so in actual words, he had left her in
no doubts as to how he viewed her appearance. Did
he honestly think that new clothes would make any
difference? She was as she was . . . and, after all, he
wasn't marrying her for her looks or her dress sense.
How galling it must be for him, though, to have to
acknowledge as his wife a plain, too thin woman like
herself. People would take one look at her and know
exactly why he had married her, and, for all his
bluntness when discussing the terms of their
marriage, she suspected that he would not want
others to know exactly why he had married her.

He left at three o'clock, telling her not to walk to
the front door with him.

He paused at the door and her heart leapt.

'Oh, I nearly forgot. You'll need a ring. I'll sort
something out. I'm involved in business meetings in
London for the rest of the week, but I should be free
on Friday. With any luck, we'll be able to finalise
the wedding arrangements then. I'll get Fiona to get
in touch with you.'

And then he was gone, the Aston leaving a cloud
of dust hanging over the drive.

# CHAPTER THREE

'LADY ELEANOR? I'm Fiona Howard, Joss's personal assistant.'

The voice was cool and self-assured, and immediately Nell pictured the woman who owned it as glossy and elegant. From her voice it was hard to define her age. She sounded sophisticated and mature, but there was also an edge of something else in her voice that warned Nell that she wasn't pleased about Joss's marriage.

In the days since their engagement had been announced she had been besieged by reporters, telephone calls and visitors, and it had been rather like being overwhelmed by a tidal wave. Only that morning one of the society magazines had telephoned, asking for a photograph to accompany their announcement, and Nell's normal calm was fast beginning to desert her.

She gripped the receiver tensely, her voice betraying her stress.

'Joss asked me to call to find out when you'll be free to go to London to buy your new clothes. I'd like a few days' warning so that I can clear my desk, and get us a hotel booking. I think we'll be able to get most of what you need in Knightsbridge, but I'm not sure what you've got in mind for the wedding dress. You'll want something simple, I expect . . .' she added with an edge of mockery under her voice that immediately made Nell take fire.

She was not going to allow this supercilious

secretary of Joss's to bully her, or to show her up as the country mouse she undoubtedly was. Generations of fighting spirit rose up inside her, and to her own surprise she heard herself saying in a voice she distinctly recognised as her formidable great-aunt's, 'That won't be necessary, Fiona. I've arranged to spend a few days with an old friend, and she'll give me all the help I need.'

There was silence from the other end of the line and then a rather curt, 'Oh, I see. Very well, then, I'll tell Joss.'

Nell had no doubt that she would, and somehow she suspected that she herself would not feature flatteringly in the telling.

Joss was coming round to see her in the evening, to bring her engagement ring and check on the progress with the arrangements. She had done very little save to check with the vicar that a Saturday four weeks hence was available for the ceremony. She knew he had been surprised by her news, but he was too polite to show it, and she also knew that her engagement was the subject of much busy speculation in the village.

When Joss came he would also want to know when she had arranged to go to Cambridge. She gnawed on her bottom lip and then picked up the phone, dialling Liz's number.

'Nell . . . how lovely . . . I haven't heard from you in ages. How are you?'

'Engaged,' she said bluntly.

There was a short pause, and then Liz said in a pleased voice, 'Oh, my dear, that nice solicitor. I am pleased.'

'No, not David,' Nell told her flatly.

'Not . . . then who?'

'Joss. Joss Wycliffe.'

There was a pause and then a quiet, 'Oh, Nell. Are you sure? I mean . . .'

'I know what you mean, Liz, and yes, I am sure, but I need your help. Clothes . . .' she added succinctly.

Liz had been before her marriage a complete clothesaholic; she also had an excellent eye for colour and line, and Nell knew that, unlike the as yet unseen Fiona, she would treat her sympathetically. If she had to have a new wardrobe, she would rather have Liz to help her choose it than anyone else.

'How many?' Liz asked crisply.

'A complete new wardrobe. Oh, and a wedding dress as well,' and for some reason she heard herself saying firmly, 'Something really stunning, Liz.'

'I know the very place; they specialise in Cinders-shall-go-to-the-ball-type things that are out of this world. Look, how soon can you get down here? I can park Lucy with Ma-in-law for a couple of days and we can concentrate totally on getting you kitted out . . . When is this wedding taking place, by the way?'

'In four weeks' time.'

There was a breathless pause and then, 'Nell, you're not . . .'

'No,' she interrupted, her breath catching high in her throat on a hysterical laugh. The thought of Joss being so overcome by desire for her that he accidentally made her pregnant was so totally unlikely that it caused her body to burn and tears to film her eyes.

'No, nothing like that . . .' she assured her friend. 'And I can come down on Monday and stay for as long as need be . . .'

'Well, a week should do it; that gives us some time

for fittings. I know how tiny you are, and whatever we buy is bound to need alterations. We're lucky down here . . . There are plenty of fabulous shops. What about attendants?'

'Only Grania, I expect, and I'm sure she'll have her own ideas on what she should wear.'

'I'm sure,' Liz agreed drily. 'But the choice isn't hers, but yours . . . I know the very thing. Pink . . . the kind of baby pink that turns her kind of skin yellow and does horrendous things to dark hair. Yes . . . I can see her in it now . . .'

'Liz,' Nell protested, but laughing despite herself. Liz had always had this effect on her, her wicked sense of humour making Nell smile even when she felt least like it. Nell could picture her now, her red hair in untidy disarray, her too wide mouth curled into a smile, her lissom body dressed in jeans and one of her husband'd discarded sweaters, and, no matter what she dressed in, nothing could disguise Liz's feminine sensuality. It was no wonder that Robert had fallen fathoms deep in love with her.

'How are the family?' she asked.

'Well, your god-daughter is fine—noisy, imposs-ible, and at times a pest, but fine . . . Jane's OK, but we're both worried about Paul. On the surface he seemed to accept our marriage very well, but there are problems at school. It can't be easy for either of them, seeing someone take their mother's place.'

'But they love you, Liz.'

'Yes, I know, and that makes it all the harder for them, poor loves. In loving me they probably feel they're betraying their mother. It's not so bad with Jane . . . I can talk to her, but Paul is just at that age when he's finding it difficult to articulate his emotions. How will you travel down?'

'I'll drive. I should arrive some time after lunch.'

'Excellent. We can spend the afternoon doing a recce and that will leave us with plenty of time on Tuesday for the serious shopping.'

It was the final wedding at Easterhay on Saturday, and so Thursday and Friday were busy with its preparation, which pleased Nell because it gave her less time to think.

Joss arrived late on Friday evening, just when she had almost given him up. Nell was in the hall when Johnson let him in. She had been arranging the last of the Michaelmas daisies in an ancient blue and white vase. She was just standing back to study her handiwork when she heard his car outside.

He came in moving with his usual lithe grace, but tonight it was underlaid by tense, restless energy. His shirt was unbuttoned at the throat, revealing corded muscles and brown skin.

'Sorry I'm late,' he apologised tersely, dropping his briefcase on to the floor. 'I got held up with a business meeting, otherwise I'd have been here after lunch.'

'Is everything all right?' Nell asked him. She had seen Joss exhibit that restless energy once or twice before, normally when he was in the throes of negotiating a new deal.

'Fine,' he responded, and then added mockingly, 'What's wrong, Nell? Hoping for a reprieve—been praying that financial disaster would overtake me, have you?'

'Why should I?' she asked, keeping her voice deliberately controlled and neutral. She had lain awake almost the whole of the previous night thinking about their future together.

Joss wasn't going to allow her to back out of this marriage, she knew that. It was imperative that he never guessed how she felt about him, and so she had decided that the safest thing she could do was to adopt a manner of cool self-control behind which she could hide her real emotions.

It was all very well to plan out in the sleepless darkness of the night what she intended to do, but now, confronted by the reality of Joss, she wondered whether she was going to be able to carry it off. His eyebrows lifted in the questioning way with which she was so familiar.

'Why should I want you to lose your money, Joss?' she asked him quietly. 'After all, I'm hardly likely to find a second millionaire willing to marry me, am I?

He gave her a narrowed look, mouth hard. 'Oh, I don't know. I suppose there must be any number of self-made men willing to buy what I'm buying from you, Nell.'

Johnson had disappeared discreetly the moment he had let Joss in, but, conscious of the fact that he could reappear at any moment, Nell said quickly, 'I wasn't sure what your plans were. It's Mrs Booth's night off, but I could make us a cold supper, if you're hungry.'

Something—was it surprise?—flashed momentairly in the golden eyes, and then he said silkily, 'How wifely of you, Nell. No, thanks, I already have a supper engagement.' She turned away quickly so that he couldn't see her face.

Of course, she should have known, given the circumstances of their coming marriage, that he would still continue seeing those other women who hung so fragilely on his arm, but somehow or other

she had managed to forget, or perhaps had
deliberately not wanted to remember that they
would continue to have their place in Joss's life.

'Of course,' she said emotionlessly, 'I should have
realised that you probably had a previous engagement.'

'Should you?' The dark eyebrows rose again. 'I
didn't realise you were telepathic, Nell, or are you
trying to tell me something else?'

She picked up the few stems of Michaelmas daisy
that she hadn't put in the vase and fidgeted with
them nervously. When he was in this kind of mood,
Joss reminded her of a caged lion, restless and also
very dangerous.

'Who exactly do you think I'm having supper
with, Nell?'

She forced herself not to betray her feelings as she
turned to look at him, deliberately curving her lips
into a remote little smile as she said quietly, 'Your
private life really isn't any concern of mine, Joss.'

To her shock, he reached out and grabbed hold of
her, his fingers encircling her wrist with painful
force. 'Isn't it?' he demanded harshly. 'By God,
Nell . . .'

He broke off abruptly when her face went white,
releasing her wrist with a mock-delicate care.

'I'm sorry,' he apologised drily. 'For a moment I
had forgotten that I am trying to turn myself into a
gentleman. How right you are to remind me, Nell.
As a lady, you won't wish to concern yourself with
the sordid details of my life, other than where it
touches upon your own. Fiona tells me that you've
arranged to go to Cambridge,' he added abruptly.

Still stunned by the bitterness she had seen and
heard, Nell said hopefully, 'Yes, I thought I'd spend

a few days with an old school-friend.'

She badly wanted to touch her wrist where he had gripped it. Her flesh ached and throbbed, and, now that the warmth of his fingers had been removed, her skin actually felt chilled.

'I thought Liz could help me refurbish my wardrobe.'

'Liz?' Joss frowned, and then his forehead cleared. 'Oh, yes, the redhead. A few days away from this place would probably do you good. I'm sorry about all the hassle you've been receiving from the Press, but only to be expected I'm afraid. I told Johnson to let me know if things threatened to get really out of hand.'

Nell stared at him. Johnson had not said anything to her about that.

'Keeping tabs on me, Joss?' she enquired bitterly. 'There's really no need, you know.'

Once again anger flared in his eyes. 'When do you plan to leave for Cambridge?' he asked tersely.

'Monday morning. I've got a wedding here tomorrow, and then there's the clearing up.'

'I'll get Audlem to take you down in the Rolls.'

'There's really no need,' Nell told him coolly. 'I'm perfectly capable of driving myself there, Joss.'

'And I'll have to see about sorting out a new car for you as well,' he added, as though she hadn't spoken. 'Is there anything particular you fancy?'

'Nothing,' she told him fiercely. 'I already have a perfectly good car, Joss. There's no need for you to buy me another one.' She emphasised the word 'buy' and he looked at her with cold eyes, a mirthless smile curling his mouth.

'Perhaps not,' he agreed, 'but it's three years since I bought the Daimler, and . . .'

Nell couldn't help it. Her face betrayed her. She cried out sharply, 'What do you mean? Gramps bought that car.'

'No, I bought it,' Joss told her.

Nell felt shaky and sick. All this time she had been driving around in a car Joss had bought, and she had never known.

'It hurts, doesn't it, Nell, to be the recipient of someone else's unwanted charity? Oh, yes, I know all about that feeling,' he told her, watching her face. 'I grew up on it, and it made me determined that one day I'd be the one doing the giving. Have you drawn up your guest list for the wedding yet?'

'Yes,' Nell told him tonelessly. 'It's in Gramps' study.' She walked into the room, knowing that Joss was following her, for once not intimidated by the sensation of having him so close to her. The list was on the desk. She picked it up and handed it to him in silence.

'Very impressive,' Joss said curtly when he had finished reading it.

'Perhaps we ought to be getting married in Westminster Abbey, not the local parish church, so that even more people can know how well you've done for yourself, Joss. Be careful, you might find they're laughing at you, not envying you.' She meant because she herself was so different from the lovely women he normally escorted, but he went white with an anger surely far out of keeping with her taunt, his eyes flat with rage and his mouth a hard, thin line.

'Laughing at me? Why, Nell? For aspiring to a higher social station than that to which I was born, because I don't have the right accent and I haven't been to the right school? Maybe I don't have those

things, but my son will, and when he's at school with
the sons of the people who are doing the laughing,
well . . . let's just see how they feel then.'

Nell was appalled at the flood of bitterness she had
released. She had had no idea that Joss felt his background so keenly, no idea how on earth to reassure
him that he was wrong, that she had never given the
supposed difference in their station a thought.

'Here,' he said curtly, reaching into his pocket
and extracting a small square box. 'You had better
have this. After all, this is the reason why I am here.'

He handed it to her, not deigning to open it
himself, but her fingers trembled over the catch of
the old velvet-covered box and she almost let it fall to
the floor. She heard Joss cursing under his breath
and then he took it from her, flipping the lid back
dexterously, so that the ring inside it caught the light
and shimmered. As he handed it back to her, she
caught her breath. She had no idea what she had
expected him to give to her as an engagement
ring—a very valuable solitaire probably, something
expensive but discreet like his own gold watch—but
this was nothing like that.

The ring was old and heavy, the gold red and
worn. The sapphire, that was it central stone,
gleamed brilliantly, diamonds surrounding it, a sea
of white fire. She stared at it in disbelief and heard
Joss saying to her, 'Don't you recognise it?'

'Recognise it?' She stared from the ring to him,
bemused, and another of his hard, cruel smiles
curled his mouth.

'You don't, do you, Nell? Has anyone ever told
you how good you are at destroying a man's ego.
Come with me.'

He led her from the study to the huge formal dining-room that was hardly ever used these days. Over the fireplace hung a portrait of the Countess of Strathmarr. She had been a Macdonald before her first marriage, and on the wrong side during the Rebellion of 1745. She had supported Bonny Prince Charlie, not just in secret with money and men, but in public in the salons of London, where she had let it be known how she felt about George of Hanover, the usurper on the English throne.

She was married at the first time at sixteen to a man older than her own father, one of the Glaswegian tobacco lords, who had died six months after the wedding, leaving his young bride immensely wealthy.

After the Rebellion had been crushed and Bonny Prince Charlie had fled, King George had the countess arrested. It had been Nell's ancestor who had saved her; one of Cumberland's men, he had fallen in love with her on sight, but in those days she had been far, far above him both in station and in wealth. Now, with her lands proscribed and her wealth filling the king's coffers and her person languishing in one of the king's prisons while she awaited trial, which would almost certainly send her to her death, Sir Henry had stepped in. Despite the fact that he strongly supported King George, he had hated the cruelties inflicted on the Highlanders, and when Cumberland praised him for his bravery during the battle of Glencoe and offered to reward the quick thinking that had saved his own life with an earldom, Sir Henry had turned it down, and requested that instead he be allowed to marry the Countess of Strathmarr.

Nell knew this story almost as well as she knew the

story of her own life. She had looked at the portrait of the young countess at least a hundred thousand times and, while she had often noticed the soft droop of her mouth and the sadness in her eyes, until Joss stood her in front of it and pointed it out to her, she had never really noticed the sapphire she was wearing on her left hand.

'She was given that ring by her tobacco lord when he married her,' Joss told her, 'and your ancestor bought it back for her from the king because it was the same colour as her eyes. Your grandfather should have given it to your grandmother, but he had to sell it to pay death-duties. How your family have suffered under that burden, Nell.'

'Like many others,' she told him quietly, but inwardly her heart was beating frantically.

'I managed to trace the ring, and I think it fitting that you should wear it as a symbol of our future together.'

Nell smiled and thanked him mechanically, but all the time her mind was on the countess and her story. How ironic that a ring that should originally have been given by her ancestor to the woman he loved should now be given to her by a man who had no feeling for her at all.

'So polite and self-controlled,' Joss mocked her. 'I shall expect more than polite words and smiles from you after you are my wife, Nell.'

'I'm not a child, Joss,' she countered. 'I know exactly what our marriage will entail, and there's really no need to hold it over me like a threat. You have already stressed that you want a son.'

'And?' Joss prompted.

'And the days are long gone when women of my class were kept ignorant and virginal until they married.'

Something leapt in the darkness of his eyes. She automatically took a step back from him.

'What are you trying to tell me, Nell?' he asked evenly.

Outside the room, the telephone in the hall rang sharply, splintering the tense silence. Glad of the excuse to escape from him, Nell opened the door and hurried to pick it up.

It was Grania, which surprised her, as her stepsister very rarely rang her up unless she wanted something.

'Nell, what on earth's going on?' she demanded sharply now. 'You can't be engaged to Joss.'

'Well, actually, I am,' Nell told her; her lips formed the words, while her mind was occupied with a hundred different thoughts. 'I'm glad you rang, Grania. The wedding will be at the end of the month, here in the village, of course. I didn't know if you'd want to be an attendent.'

'How brave of you, darling,' Grania trilled at the other end of the line. 'I suppose I shall have to be, shan't I? I promise I shall try not to outshine you. Is Joss there, by the way?' she added lightly. 'He left some papers here at my flat the other night when he came round.' Nell stiffened, remembering how she had once thought that Joss's visits to her grandfather might be because he hoped to marry her stepsister.

'He is here,' she said distantly. 'I'll just put him on to you.'

She handed the receiver to Joss and turned away blindly, but she had hardly taken three steps before Joss was replacing the instrument.

'Don't go, Nell,' he demanded. 'We haven't finished our discussion.'

'I'm afraid I must,' she said coolly. 'I've got

rather a lot to do for this wedding tomorrow, and you did say something about having a supper date.'

'How cool you are, Nell. Cool and remote like a rarefied atmosphere. What will you do when I take you to my bed? I wonder. Close your eyes and tell yourself that you are doing it for the sake of the family?'

It hurt that he should think her so incapable of normal feelings and emotions, but, even as the muscles cramped with the pain controlling her reaction to his words, she knew that to deny them was the most dangerous thing she could do. So instead she offered him a brief, tormented smile.

'You're the one who proposed this marriage, Joss,' she reminded him. 'If you've changed your mind . . .'

'No . . . and neither will you change yours. Remember that, Nell,' he warned her as he walked to the door. 'You are committed to me now. And if you try to avoid that commitment, I shan't rest until I've found you.'

As he left, she found herself feeling almost sorry for him. Poor Joss, how desperately he must want a son to inherit her grandfather's title.

She marvelled at the lengths to which such a need could drive a man, especially a man of Joss's intelligence, and then went sadly back to the study and checked on the details for the morning's wedding.

# CHAPTER FOUR

'YOU'VE arrived at last. Come on in and let me have a look at you.'

Extricating herself from her friend's hug, Nell walked with her up the path. Liz's home was several miles outside Cambridge, an untidy, rambling rectory she and her husband were half-way through renovating. It had a large garden with herbaceous borders, almost totally overgrown with weeds, and Liz's little girl lay asleep in a pram, under an apple tree in the back garden.

'She's just gone down,' Liz told Nell. 'So we've got at least an hour to chat and I want to hear everything,' she told her friend warningly, 'and I do mean everything. You and Joss—honestly, Nell, I can hardly believe it even now. How long has it been going on? I had no idea the two of you were involved. What a dark horse you are,' she said affectionately.

'We're not—involved, I mean,' Nell said flatly. 'It's what you might call a marriage of convenience.'

'What?' Liz put down the coffee-jug that she was filling with water and stared at her friend.

'It's a business arrangement, Liz,' Nell told her doggedly. 'Joss is marrying me because he wants the family name and the house, and because he hopes that one day our son will inherit Gramps' title, and I'm marrying him because it means I can keep my home and the staff.'

'A marriage of convenience. Good heavens!' Liz

exclaimed in a failing voice, goggling at her. 'How very Georgette Heyer.' And then, more seriously when she saw Nell's face, she said, 'Nell, are you sure? When you told me you were engaged, I felt sure it could only be because you were head over heels in love, knowing you the way I do.'

'I am,' Nell told her painfully. 'I love Joss, but I know he doesn't love me.'

'Oh, Nell.' Liz put down the coffee-jug and came over to her putting her arms round her. 'Oh, my dear, are you sure you know what you're doing? Life isn't like a novel, you know, with the hero falling madly in love with the heroine after he marries her. Do you really know what you're letting yourself in for?'

'Yes,' Nell told her bleakly. 'Don't worry. I'm not a complete idiot, Liz. I know quite well Joss is never going to fall in love with me.'

'Oh, Nell, I wish you'd reconsider,' Liz said sitting down beside her. 'I know you. You may be able to cope now, but are you going to cope in the years to come?'

'I'll find a way,' Nell told her.

'Must you go through with it?' Liz pleaded.

Nell looked at her. 'Yes, I have to.'

She saw the look on her friend's face and smiled. 'No, Liz, nothing like that. But when Gramps died I promised him that I'd do everything that I could to keep the house and the estate in the family.'

'A deathbed promise,' Liz derided. 'Oh, Nell, how could he do that to you?'

'Liz, please,' Nell protested, her voice wavering slightly. 'My mind's made up.'

And, seeing the anguish in her eyes, Liz sighed. 'Very well. I won't say another word. Oh, Nell, marriage can be hard, even when you are in love with one another. I hate to think what it's going to be like for you.'

'I'll manage,' Nell told her, and as she moved her hand Liz caught sight of her engagement ring for the first time, her eyes widening. In awe, she stared at it.

Glad to be able to change the subject, Nell told her the story of it.

'Good heavens, how romantic,' Liz exclaimed. 'Nell, are you sure he doesn't love you?'

'Positive,' Nell told her drily. 'He probably bought the ring thinking it would be an excellent thing for our son to hand it over to his bride one day.'

'It's a shame that it's still not possible to buy a peerage from a poor, hard-up king,' Liz commented. 'I tend to forget your title most of the time, Lady Eleanor,' she teased.

A car arrived outside and Liz dashed to the window. 'It's Robert's mother,' she told Nell. 'She promised she'd come round this afternoon and babysit for us so that we could go out and do the recce.'

'What about Jane and Paul?'

'Jane's going home with a friend after school, and as for Paul . . .' She sighed faintly. 'Paul's staying with his aunt in Gloucester for a few days. He's going through a very difficult patch at the moment, Nell. There've been problems at school. Complaints that he's taken to bullying some of the younger boys, and that just isn't like him. He has nightmares as well. Poor boy, I wish I could do something to help, but Robert thinks the best possible thing for him at the moment is a complete change of scene. Ellen is

his mother's sister, and she's always had a soft spot
for him. She and her husband don't have any
children of their own and he'd be able to respond to
her spoiling in the way that he can't respond to mine
at the moment, because there'd be no guilt attached
to it.'

How wise and compassionate her friend was, Nell
reflected while she was introduced to Liz's mother-
in-law, a pleasant, plump woman in her late fifties.

'We shouldn't be more than a couple of hours,'
Liz told her mother-in-law.

'Don't you worry. Take just as long as you like,'
she smiled.

'Now——' Liz began as she emerged breathlessly
from her car, having parked it in the centre of
Cambridge. Nell had had to wait several minutes
while she had gathered together all her belongings,
and then another few seconds when she remembered
that she had put her car keys in her handbag and to
get them out so that she could lock the car.

Liz had always been like this, slightly dizzy and
disorganised.

'I know exactly where we're going for your
wedding dress,' Liz informed her, 'so we'll leave
that for today. What I need to know now is exactly
how much wardrobe renovation is taking place.'

'Joss wants me to replace everything,' Nell told
her flatly. 'Apparently my existing clothes don't fit
in with the image he wants his wife to portray.'

If she expected Liz to sympathise with her, she
was disappointed.

'Let's face it,' Liz said brutally, 'they don't fit in
with any image other than the outdated one of a
spinster schoolmarm. Honestly, Nell, with your
figure you could wear anything. Why on earth you

hide it in those awful sweaters and baggy skirts, I'll never know.'

'They're good quality,' Nell protested mildly. 'I can't afford to spend money on fashions, Liz, you know that.'

'Who's talking about fashion?' Liz demanded. 'You could go into Marks and Spencer any day of the week and come out with at least half a dozen outfits smarter than the one you're wearing, and just as good quality. What about the honeymoon? What will you need for that?'

Nell stared at her. 'I've no idea,' she admitted. 'Joss hasn't mentioned a honeymoon.'

Liz's eyebrows rose. 'Since your husband-to-be stipulated a complete new wardrobe, we'd better oblige him, hadn't we? What sort of life will you be leading once you're married, Nell?'

'I'm not really sure. I expect Joss will want us to do a certain amount of entertaining, and then there'll be business dinners, that kind of thing.'

'And the local social scene . . .' Liz prodded. 'Hunt balls, charity dos?'

'Well, yes,' Nell agreed.

'Mm . . . I think I'm beginning to get the picture. Pity we didn't keep your car and driver,' she added with a grin. Despite Nell's protests, Joss had had his way and she had been driven down to Liz's in his Rolls by his chauffeur. 'I rather like the idea of a uniformed chauffeur driving behind us in a Rolls-Royce, picking up our packages, don't you?'

She saw Nell's face and laughed.

'Poor Nell, but I do so enjoy teasing you. Ah . . . now here's a shop that will be well worth a visit,' she exclaimed, directing Nell's attention to a double-fronted shop tucked away down a small alley. 'They specialise in really good quality German separates, Mondi, Escarder, that kind of thing.'

She saw Nell's blank look and laughed again. 'You'll like them,' she promised her. 'Escarder is very elegant, very county. Mondi's younger, more fun. Both are extremely well-made and hard-wearing. We can go in now and have a look, if you like—get your eye in, so to speak.'

The shop was much larger than it appeared from the outside, taking up two floors and stretching quite a way back. The extent of the Mondi range of separates stunned Nell, who had been visualising one or two skirts and perhaps half a dozen or so shirts and sweaters to go with them. Instead she was confronted by a bewildering array of colours, styles and designs.

'This red would look good on you,' Liz exclaimed, reaching for a beautiful stitched-down pleated skirt.

'I never wear red,' Nell protested. 'I'm far too pale.'

'Nonsense,' Liz told her. 'This skirt and I think this blouse and oh . . . definitely this sweater.'

Ignoring Nell's protests, she turned to smile at the assistant, quickly explaining what she had in mind, and before she could say a word Nell found she was being hustled into an immaculate changing-room with a smiling assistant behind her.

The skirt, in the smallest size they had, did look surprisingly good on her, its neat lines accentuating her slender shape. The soft wool blouse felt lovely against her skin, although she did try to murmur a protest when the sales girl offered her the sweater that Liz had chosen. It was the same bright red as the skirt, with a design appliquéd on it, and was

surely far too young for her. The sales girl persuaded
her to try it on.

As soon as she was outside and being paraded for
Liz's critical inspection, she realised she was fighting
a losing battle. While the sales girl and Liz discussed
alterations and timescale, Nell glanced round the
shop. In the mirror on the other side of the room, she
could see someone wearing the same outfit as her.
On this other woman it looked stunning; the pleated
skirt falling gently to mid-calf, accentuating the
tiny, delicate ankle bones, the red warming her pale
skin.

It was only when Liz spoke to her and she turned
her head, the movement setting the pleats swirling,
that Nell realised that the woman in the mirror was
herself.

'What are you looking so bemused about?' Liz
questioned her, but Nell wouldn't tell her.
However, seeing herself like that and not realising
who she was had given her confidence a well-needed
boost, and once the first outfit had been decided
upon she found it astonishingly easy to agree with
Liz that she must have the grey Escarder outfit, and
that the very dark blue suit, with the tiny velvet
collar and fitted jacket, would be ideal for any formal
lunches she might attend.

Sweaters, scarves, belts, even jewellery, all added
to what seemed to be a huge pile of things on the
table in front of them. In addition to the bright red
Mondi outfit, she chose another, but this time it was
her own choice, although both Liz and the sales girl
instantly approved: a very neat, straight skirt that
would have to be shortened in a very dark, greeny-
bluey-grey non-colour with a toning knitted tabard
in a pale dove-grey. It had an attractive button

detail at the back, which the sales girl told her would
have to be taken in to hang properly over her very
slim hips. There was even a jacket to go with it:
dove-grey again, cut on the bias, with a tiny
mandarin collar and the kind of shape that
made it swing out around her with every step she
took.

'That's a fabulous start,' Liz approved, when
they were outside in the street again. 'But it is only a
start,' she warned Nell. 'You're going to need a
good top coat, a raincoat and boots, not to mention
evening clothes, and then, just in case Joss does take
you away on a honeymoon, you're going to need
beachwear.' She gave Nell a very direct look. 'Not
to mention all those other things that brides always
buy for their honeymoon, Nell.'

Nell's eyes met hers in startled comprehension.
She started to shake her head, but before she could
make a denial Liz said practically, 'Look, I'm not
suggesting anything particularly exotic, or frivolous,
but I always feel extra specially good when I've got
new undies to go under my new clothes. There's a
small shop, not far from here, that specialises in
exactly the kind of thing that you'll like.' She
glanced at her watch. 'We haven't got time to go
today, and tomorrow morning I want to take you to
the dress shop where I think you'd be able to get
your wedding dress. We might be able to fit it in
after that. Thank goodness for mother-in-law,' she
added in a heartfelt voice as she led the way to her
parked car.

They were just ten minutes over the two hours Liz
had promised when they got back to the house.
Lucy, her little girl, had just woken up and was
sitting placidly on her grandmother's knee. When

she saw her mother, her face broke into a beaming smile and she stretched out chubby little arms towards her.

'Here you are, you hold her for me for a moment, godmamma, while I show Joan out to her car,' Liz told her, dumping the little girl in Nell's arms.

She felt surprisingly heavy to Nell, who hadn't held her since the christening. That had been over eight months ago, and she had grown a good deal since then.

Liz had rung her to tell her proudly less than a month ago that she was already starting to walk, and Nell experienced evidence of this as she squirmed in her arms, obviously wanting to be put down. She was just starting to get fractious when Liz came back in.

'She's a darling,' Nell told Liz honestly.

'Sometimes,' Liz agreed with a smile, 'and at others . . .' She pulled a face and Nell laughed. 'Wait until you've got one of your own, Nell, then you'll know exactly what I mean. Will you and Joss try for a family straight away?' she asked frankly, deftly holding Lucy in one arm while she started to prepare a meal for her with her free hand. 'All right then, you can go down,' she told her squirming daughter, 'but only in your playpen.'

The moment she was on the floor, Lucy struggled to her feet, holding on to the frame of her playpen and then beaming in delight. She teetered unsteadily on her toes.

'I expect so,' Nell confirmed. 'After all, one of the main reasons Joss is marrying me is because he wants a son.'

'How will you cope with that, Nell?' Liz asked her gently, turning to face her. They had been friends

for a long time and, as teenagers, had had no secrets
from one another. Nell had been the recipient of all
Liz's outpourings as she first fell in love with
Robert, and so she didn't resent the question. What
she was desperately hoping was that Joss's indifference to her would enable her to retain her own
cool reserve. Any physical intimacy between them
would be an act of procreation, not an act of desire.

She had no fear that Joss would hurt her in any
way or force her. She suspected that sexually he was
extremely experienced and probably extremely
skilled. It would be in his own interests, as much as
hers, to make it easy for her to accept him as her
lover.

These were uncomfortable thoughts and best not
dwelt on, Nell told herself firmly, a decision which
she stuck to resolutely while she helped Liz to bath
Lucy and then put her to bed.

Robert arrived home just after seven o'clock,
greeting his wife with a warm hug and a kiss, and
Nell with a smile.

She had only met him on a handful of previous
occasions: the wedding, Lucy's christening and then
on a couple of brief visits when she had been able to
get away for a few days, but Nell had taken to him
on sight. He was a good counterweight for her
volatile friend and, having married young the first
time while still at medical school, at thirty-three he
was only seven years older then Liz.

Nell tried to make the excuse that she had things to
do in her room to give them some time on their own,
but Liz laughed, seeing through her subterfuge, and
telling her with a grin that included her husband,
'Nell, Robert will be only too pleased to sneak off
into the sitting-room and have a quiet drink and

relax. Believe me, he hates it when I bombard him with chatter the moment he walks in the door.'

She made a face and laughed, but Nell could see from Robert's slightly shamefaced expression that her friend wasn't completely exaggerating.

Dinner was an easygoing affair, eaten without formality in the small, sunny breakfast-room off the kitchen.

'One day, when I've got the house organised properly, we'll be able to eat in the dining-room,' Liz promised, and then it was Robert's turn to tease his wife, asking if Nell had yet seen the havoc she had wreaked upstairs.

'I started decorating the bedrooms,' she explained to Nell defensively,' and then when I became pregnant with Lucy the smell of paint made me feel so terrible that I had to stop.'

'Ah, yes, but what she doesn't tell you is that she was decorating *all* the bedrooms,' Robert added slyly.

'I've finished one of them,' Liz countered with an air of injured martyrdom. 'That's the one you're in, Nell.'

Nell had already admired the pretty lemon and blue colour scheme. Liz had always been deft with her needle, and the soft furnishings in the room gave evidence that she had retained her skill. The walls had been sponged in a pretty shade of lemon on white and a stencilled ribbon border applied at cornice-level.

'The walls in this house are so bumpy that traditional wallpaper is out of the question,' Liz confided. 'I went on one of these three-day decorative painting courses, Nell. I really enjoyed it. You should try them. Think of the money you'll be able to save Joss if you do your own decorating,' she added wickedly.

Nell laughed, but in reality she was aching inside. She and Joss would never share the camaraderie and love so very evident between her friend and her husband . . . She would never have the pleasure of lovingly decorating their home.

Joss would probably insist on the most expensive interior designers, and he would probably tell her that he was sending Fiona out to choose the colour schemes, she thought acidly.

'You wouldn't realise it to see her sitting there looking sweet as milk,' she heard Liz telling her husband, 'but when we were at school together, Nell could be as stubborn as the proverbial mule when she wanted to be.'

Stubborn . . . Yes, perhaps sometimes she could be, Nell allowed, and it struck her that if she was not to be totally swamped in her marriage with Joss she was going to have to re-activate that stubbornness and hold out for her own rightful say in those decisions that affected them jointly.

The redecoration of the house was a case in point. Although he hadn't actually spelled it out to her, Nell had sensed that, once the house was redecorated, Joss would want to show it off to his business colleagues and friends, but she was damned if she was going to allow him to turn her home into a larger version of the soulless, glossy place where he lived now.

If that was Joss's idea of how a home should look, well then, she was going to have to let him know that it wasn't hers.

'Come back,' Liz teased her. 'Where were you?'

'Redecorating,' Nell admitted with a smile. 'I

think I'm going to need to pick your brains a little, Liz. Joss wants the house redoing, and I suspect our ideas are going to clash. I want to make sure I'm fully armed before I tackle him about it. Any suggestions?'

Liz had, plus a list of contracts and firms who specialised in period work.

The two of them spent the whole evening discussing the merits of restoring what was already there and replacing what wasn't to lift the rather gloomy Victorian air from the house and yet keep its unique character.

Nell went to bed feeling happier than she had done since Joss had asked her to marry him. Talking with Liz had restored her self-confidence and made her see how those last months with her grandfather had worn her down and suppressed her natural exuberance for life.

Her future was in her own hands. She could put aside her love for Joss and make their relationship work on a business footing, devoting herself to their family and the estate, developing her own interests and acting as Joss's hostess whenever he required, thus building her own individual life that would barely impinge on his; or she could let herself dwell on her feelings for him, and succumb to the self-pity she sensed lying in wait for her, and in doing so become an object of contempt, to herself as much to anyone else.

It was gone midnight when she went to bed, but her mood of optimism didn't last. No sooner was she tucked up beneath Liz's beautifully appliquéd duvet cover than her mind began to torment her. How would she cope with the reality of having Joss as her lover, while at the same time knowing that he didn't *love* her? Would she be strong enough to subdue her own responses, to force her reactions to be those of a distant, passionless stranger? Because that was what she would have to do.

Once she allowed her true feelings to break through her defences, she wasn't going to be able to stop herself from revealing the truth to Joss. Their marriage would be easier for her to endure if there was no physical aspect to it, but Joss wanted a son. And she too wanted children.

'Come on, sleepy-head, we've got a lot to do today.'

Guiltily Nell struggled through the layers of sleep that had engulfed her with the dawn, to find Liz standing beside her bed holding a mug of coffee.

'Oh, Liz,' she murmured contritely, 'I'm so sorry. How awful of me. You shouldn't have brought me a drink . . . you've got far too much to do.'

'Not this morning,' Liz told her cheerfully. 'Ma-in-law arrived early and swooped up Lucy, so we've got the whole day to ourselves. However, it might be a good idea to make an early start.'

Within an hour they were on the road, Nell at Liz's persuasion wearing one of her new outfits—the red one, since the skirts for the others were being shortened.

'We'll have to do something about your hair,' Liz told her forthrightly as she parked in Cambridge.

It was a clear autumn day, crisp and warm in the sun here in Cambridge, but during the drive they had passed fields in which the mist lay thick and white, and the weathermen were forecasting frost by the end of the week.

This was far from the first time that Liz had

commented on her hair-style, and Nell touched her plaits defensively.

'I need something that's easy to look after, Liz. My hair's so straight and fine.'

'I agree . . . but I've made you an appointment with my hairdresser for a consultation. You'll want a different style to go with your wedding dress, anyway,' she reminded her.

This was all news to Nell, but nevertheless she followed Liz docilely while she led her into an almost frighteningly sterile-looking hair-salon.

Paul, the stylist, was bearded and older then Nell had expected. His smile eased some of her apprehension, but when he unwound her plaits and studied her hair, she found herself saying shakily, 'I don't want it cut.'

'I should think not,' he agreed, 'but if I could suggest a trim of the ends, and then we can talk about the kind of options that are open to you. Long hair is very "in" at the moment, and there are several different styles I can think of that would suit you.'

He gave her some books to study while her hair was shampooed.

The women in them looked impossibly glamorous and soignée, and never in a lifetime could Nell imagine her hair looking like theirs, but when she and Liz stepped out of the salon into the autumn sunshine just over an hour later, she was forced to confess that Paul had practically performed a miracle.

Her hair was drawn sleekly back into her nape, revealing the delicacy of her face. He had twisted her hair into a soft chignon, which was now confined in a pretty snood. A bright red bow secured the snood and picked up the colour of her outfit, and Nell had been forced to admit that the style was so easy that she should have no trouble copying it herself. And it looked . . . well, it looked a world away from her normal plaits.

'For the wedding . . . well, we shall see when you have chosen your dress,' Paul had told her, 'but I have a couple of ideas in mind.' And she and Liz had been forced to be content with that, promising to return once the dress had been chosen.

He had even given her a small leaflet showing several easy styles for long hair; all of them stunningly chic and yet amazingly simple to achieve, and although Nell herself didn't realise it there was a new spring to her step as she walked alongside her friend.

'If you must wear your hair in a plait, then I suggest this,' Paul had told her, demonstrating a style that gathered her hair into one plait which he then doubled lengthways and decorated with a large bow.

'This is the kind of style you can wear with jeans. A country style,' he had told her.

Liz had burst out laughing, saying,

'I doubt that Nell has ever owned a pair of jeans in her life, have you, Nell?' She hadn't. Her grandfather and her aunt had never approved of women in trousers. A heavy tweed skirt with flat, fur-lined boots had been her winter wear for tramping the estate, but now Liz was already talking about the rival merits of various styles of jeans, promising her that before she left Cambridge she would have several pairs in her luggage.

Liz had also made an appointment for them at the wedding-dress salon, and the owner herself welcomed them inside. She was a pretty girl in her mid-twenties, with dark brown curly hair, and an efficient manner.

'Nothing too fussy,' Nell told her nervously, as she offered them both seats.

'Don't listen to her,' Liz chimed in. 'This is going to be some wedding and she's going to be its star . . . You had the most heavenly satin creation in the window the other day . . .'

To Nell's relief, Susan Marchant shook her head.

'It is lovely, but it would dwarf you,' she explained to Nell. 'I've got something in mind . . . but it's rather different from the type of dress that's popular at the moment.'

She went to one of the glass cases and withdrew a white linen dress bag, unzipping the cover and revealing the dress.

'It's Italian,' she added, hanging it so that they could see it properly.

'Oh, Nell,' Liz breathed, 'it's fantastic.'

And it was. White silk jersey, embroidered with crystals and pearls, cut in the simplest of twenties style and ankle-length, the hem fringed and slightly higher to one side than the other.

'It's the tiniest size, but I think ideal for you,' she told Nell. 'Would you like to try it on?'

Nell nodded, her mouth dry.

Tiny shoestring straps supported the dress, the bareness of her skin shadowed by an almost translucent silk top that covered her shoulders and upper arms.

The dress was unbelievably heavy, and a perfect fit, right down to its length. As she walked into the room to show it to Liz, the light caught the embroidery, dazzling the eye. When she moved, the silk jersey moved sensuously with her.

It was a dream of a dress, and when she looked at her reflection in the mirror. Nell had to caution herself against the folly of aching to have Joss turn and look at her in it, his eyes warm with love and desire.

But she would never see that hot leap of need in Joss's eyes—at least, not for herself.

'Of course you'll have to have a different hair-style,' Susan was saying practically. 'Something pre-Raphaelite, I would suggest, and perhaps just a simple wreath of fresh flowers . . .'

'Oh no . . . I'm too old,' Nell protested, but both Susan and Liz swept her objections aside, and somehow or other she found herself giving way to them.

They left the salon just in time to have a late lunch at a popular wine bar, full of well-groomed young men and women, most of them a little too old to be undergraduates. Liz told Nell that they were probably involved in one way or another in the computer industry that had boomed in Cambridge in the sixties.

After lunch she insisted on taking her to several more small shops, and by four o'clock they had to make a trip back to the car to rid themselves of their carrier bags, and Nell's new wardrobe had swelled considerably, to include three pairs of jeans, and casual tops to go with them, another dressy suit, two dresses which could be dressed up or down, and two evening dresses, including one in black velvet that fitted her like a glove and had a soft silk satin frill that started at the hips and dipped to an attractive V at the front and back, the back V adorned with a bow that formed a provocative bustle, the satin then frilling gently down to the hemline.

'Just shoes, accessories and undies tomorrow,' Liz puffed as they unloaded their purchases. 'And now, I think, back to Paul, to consult him about your wedding-day hair-style.'

'I can hardly come all the way here to have my hair done,' Nell protested, but Liz was adamant.

'No, but he can show you the kind of style you should have.' And rather reluctantly Nell found herself retracing her footsteps to the salon.

Paul knew exactly what style she should have. He showed her a photograph of a young woman with a mass of artlessly waved long hair that floated around her like a veil. It was exactly right for the dress, but surely far too exotic for her?

'Not at all . . . Look, come in tomorrow morning first thing and I'll show you. Maria, the make-up artist, is in tomorrow,' he added casually. 'Why not have a consultation with her at the same time?'

Nell wanted to protest, but she could see that Liz was not going to let her, and so recklessly she agreed. After all, since she appeared to have stepped into an unreal Alice-in-Wonderland-type world, why not simply let the flow carry her with it?

It had been years since she had spent her time so self-indulgently, and she was discovering that she quite enjoyed it. It was a little unnerving to rediscover this unexpected sybaritic streak, and as they hurried back to the car Liz noticed with fond amusement that her friend was already walking with a jauntier step, almost subconsciously preening herself when they drew second looks from other people. And why not? Nell had stood in the shadow of her flamboyant stepsister for too long. It was her nature to give generously of her time and her self, and in Liz's opinion she had allowed her grandfather to impose dreadfully upon her.

Initially when Nell had told her what she was doing she had been horrified, dreading how the kind of marriage Nell had described to her would affect someone of her friend's extra-sensitive nature, but now she was beginning to think that it was the best thing that could have happened to her. Already Nell seemed to have grown, to have rediscovered those facets of her personality that had been suppressed during the years of living with her grandfather; already she was developing new strengths.

She realised suddenly that Nell had fallen behind, and looked back to see that her friend had paused outside a shop selling antique china and glass.

'Fabulous, arent they?' Liz sighed 'But out of the question for me. Can you imagine what havoc two teenagers and a baby would wreak on this little lot?'

'That dinner service is exactly like one at home, only ours is more complete . . .'

Liz frowned as she stared at the item in question. In her opinion it was rather ugly, being very ornate and rich, the white china decorated with a gold-leaf frieze and dark purple bands.

'Are you thinking of buying it?' she asked Nell cautiously.

Nell laughed. 'No, I think it's horrible. I was just wondering, though . . .' She bit her lip and looked directly at her friend. 'Liz, you know that Joss is paying for all my new clothes . . . and the wedding. I hate that . . .' She looked away, all her joy in her new things draining from her. 'I was just wondering how much they were selling this service for, and if it was worth trying to sell ours . . .'

'Can you do that?' Liz asked her.

'Oh, yes. Gramps left the house and all its

contents to me . . . I must admit I'd reached the point of wondering about having the more valuable items of furniture valued, but many of them were designed especially for the house, and they are family heirlooms, but this dinner service is Victorian and nothing like as pretty as the Sèvres one . . .'

She smiled as she caught sight of Liz's startled expression and said apologetically. 'Yes, I know that is worth much more, but it's lovely, and I couldn't bring myself to sell it; but this . . . It would be so marvellous to tell Joss I can buy my own clothes . . .'

'Well, there's only one way to find out' Liz told her briskly. 'Let's go inside.'

Half an hour later they both emerged from the shop, dazed. It had turned out that the dinner service in the window had been sold to an American who had fallen desperately in love with it. A telephone call to the hotel where she was staying had elicited the information that she would be more than pleased to buy an additional service, since her dining-room sat thirty. The price agreed had made Nell's mind spin. Perhaps it was only a drop in the ocean if set against the death-duties . . . but to have several thousand pounds at her disposal . . . to be able to tell Joss that she could buy her clothes herself . . .

Arrangements had been made for the dealer to call and inspect the service, and it had been agreed that if everything was satisfactory the deal would go through.

'A very satisfactory day all round,' Liz exclaimed happily an hour later when she and Nell were sitting in her kitchen playing with the baby who had just been returned by her doting grandmother. 'What time will you have to leave tomorrow?'

'Mid to late afternoon, Joss said. He's going to

send Audlem and the Rolls to collect me.'

'Well, that gives us enough time to collect the alterations, and do everything else, but we'll need another early start.'

Nell groaned, and her friend laughed unsympathetically.

# CHAPTER FIVE

DESPITE the very severe lecture Nell had given herself, telling herself she was being extremely foolish, she couldn't quite suppress the tiny quiver of pleasure that ran through her when she studied her reflection in the bedroom mirror, prior to Joss's chauffeur's arrival.

Liz had persuaded her to change into some of her new separates to travel home in, and there was no doubt about it; the sludge-green and dove-grey outfit, so potentially dull when described, looked stunning against the paleness of her skin and hair, adding a fragile, ethereal quality to her features that made her study them in vague surprise.

'You look fabulous,' Liz pronounced, coming in to check on her progress. 'All you need now is a touch of that new eyeshadow and . . .'

Nell sighed faintly, wondering if she had been quite mad to allow Liz to persuade her into buying so much new make-up. It had been one thing when the girl in the salon applied it, but to achieve the same effect herself . . .

'It's easy,' Liz promised her, reading her mind. 'All you need is a little bit of self-confidence.'

'And an awful lot of skill,' Nell finished for her.

Liz laughed.

'Not an *awful* lot . . . I promise you, it isn't that difficult, Nell. Watch . . .'

It certainly didn't seem it, but Nell still felt dubious about being able to achieve for herself the same magical transformation of her features that Liz had wrought.

When she said as much, Liz said wickedly, 'Do you know, Nell, I've always itched to do this . . . to make you shine in your true colours, instead of hiding yourself away behind that mask you use . . . I know you feel you can't hold a candle to Grania, but that's nonsense.'

'Liz, I *can't* compete with Grania,' Nell objected, interrupting her.

'You *aren't* competing,' Liz told her gently. 'You are yourself, Nell, in your own way every bit as attractive as Grania, and in my opinion a darn sight more lovable. You've got everything, haven't you?' she added briskly, seeing that she was embarrassing her friend. 'I'll come to you a couple of days before the wedding, and I'll bring the dress . . . You'll organise something for Grania to wear, will you?'

She broke off as she heard a car, going over to the window and looking out.

'Wow, I love the Rolls,' she exclaimed. 'It might be rather a conspicuous example of life's goodies, but it definitely has a certain something . . .' She paused and then said incredulously, 'Nell, I thought you said Joss was sending his chauffeur for you . . .'

'Yes, he is,' Nell agreed, a hard knot of agitation suddenly twisting her stomach.

'Well, he hasn't. He's come for you himself.'

'Probably to make sure I don't try to renege on our arrangement,' Nell told her quickly, suppressing an instinctive urge to rush over to the window and see for herself that her friend was right. Her stomach was doing somersaults, and she had to give herself a very severe lecture, reminding herself of exactly why it was that Joss was marrying her, and warning herself that if she was going to react like this just at the thought of seeing him then she was going to have a hard time maintaining her supposed indifference to him once they were actually married.

'Come on. We'd better go down,' Liz urged her.

Although she had only met Joss on a couple of previous occasions, it was Liz who greeted him with an easy warmth that Nell envied, welcoming him in with a smile and a friendly kiss of congratulation on one lean cheek.

'Nell told us you were sending your chauffeur for her,' she commented as she led the way to her sunny kitchen.

'That *was* my intention,' Joss agreed carelessly, 'but I found I had a free afternoon, so I decided to drive down myself.'

Just being in the same room with him was making Nell's head spin. He was dressed casually in jeans, the neck of his checked shirt open beneath his sweater; he looked fit and healthy, a man more used to living outdoors than working in an office, his skin tanned and moulded firmly to his bones. Every movement he made was lithely efficient; he didn't fidget when he sat down, or betray any of the other nervous mannerisms Nell knew were hers. In fact, he looked as though he felt more at home in Liz's kitchen then she did herself.

'Well, now that you *are* here, why don't you both stay and have dinner with us?'

Nell knew he would refuse. He must obviously want to spend as little time in her company as possible. Once they were married, she expected she would barely see him.

'Marvellous, but insist on being allowed to take you and Robert out. Can you recommend anywhere good locally?'

So far he had done no more than merely acknowledge her presence, Nell reflected, listening to the brief argument between Liz and himself as to who ought to pay for dinner. He won, as Nell had known he would . . . What had she been expecting? That he would take one look at her in her new clothes and be transfixed with amazement at the change in her?

'Shopping all done?' he asked her at length, turning to look at her.

'I think so.'

Why on earth did she have to sound so strained and tense? She was behaving like a piqued child, betraying to a man of his sharp intelligence the very thing she wanted to conceal.

'Oh, we've done marvellously well,' Liz told him, coming to her rescue.

'Yes,' he agreed, giving Nell a narrow-eyed look. 'I can see that. Congratulations.'

'Don't congratulate me,' Liz told him, instantly nettled. 'It wasn't very difficult. After all, I did have excellent raw material.'

To Nell's astonishment, Joss said urbanely, 'I agree. And I wasn't congratulating you on the effect you've achieved, but merely on persuading Nell to allow the transformation to take place. My wife-to-be possesses an extraordinarily determined stubborn streak upon occasions.'

'So do most women if they think they're in danger of being treated like doormats,' Liz returned crisply.

Joss's eyebrows rose and he looked directly at Nell. 'Is that what you think, Nell? That I'm going to treat you like a doormat?'

To her horror, she flushed uncomfortably and couldn't meet his eyes. 'No, of course not,' she told him in a husky voice.

'Good. Because I certainly intend that our partnership shall start off on an even footing. Of course, which one of us manages to wrest a major share of it from the other during the course of our marriage remains to be seen.'

A subtle threat to warn her that *he* intended to be the dominant partner in their marraige? If so, it was unnecessary; she already knew it, and he had an advantage he didn't even dream yet that he possessed. That he would *never* know that he posssessed, if she had anything to do with it.

The four of them dined at a small local restaurant which Liz had recommended.

To judge from the others' appetites, the food was excellent, but Nell barely touched hers. She still wasn't at ease in Joss's company; she didn't feel engaged to him . . . didn't feel as though she was going to become his wife. She turned her head slightly and studied him out of the corner of her eye.

Robert and Liz were talking and, under cover of their conversation, Joss said quietly to her, 'What's wrong? Checking to make sure I'm using the right cutlery?'

Colour stung her face. 'No,' she told him in a choked voice.

'It's all right, Nell,' he told her quietly. 'You needn't keep watching me like an anxious sheepdog. Poor Nell,' he mocked her. 'Life's full of unexpected pitfalls, isn't it?'

Before she could say anything, Robert had broken off his conversation with Liz to address Joss, and soon the two men were engaged in a discussion of their differing childhoods.

Robert had been brought up by elderly parents and had rebelled by leaving home as young as he could to go to medical school.

'Of course, I was wildly out of my depth. I thought I was adult, but in fact I was totally naïve. I look around me at some of the kids I see today. They're terrifyingly adult. Too adult. I don't envy them.'

'I grew up in the tenements of Glasgow,' Joss told them, 'as I'm sure Nell has already told you.' He looked sharply at her, but Nell said nothing. 'My mother was sixteen when I was conceived. My father the same age. I was brought up by my grandparents and I was only two years younger than my grandmother's youngest child.

'My mother left home when she was eighteen. She's living in Canada now . . . married with children. We keep in touch in a desultory sort of fashion, but there's no real closeness between us. My father was killed in a motorbike accident when I was five.

'My grandmother had eight children while I was growing up, and my grandfather was out of work. I ran wild . . . despite the thrashings I got from my grandfather. I was lucky enough though to have a schoolteacher who thought he saw a glimmer of intelligence behind the belligerence. He . . .'

Nell blinked away the tears threatening to blur her vision.

She could picture him so easily; a small, lonely, aggressive little boy, dirty and perhaps a little scruffy, treating life with defiance because it was his only means of defence.

'Not hungry, Nell?' he asked her.

She gave him a wan smile.

'Wedding nerves, I expect,' Robert interrupted. 'I suffered from them myself. In fact, I lost so much weight that after we were married, Liz nearly had to carry *me* over the threshold.'

They all laughed but Nell felt drained and tired, and she wanted the evening to come to an end.

If she was honest with herself, she had to admit that she was envious of her friends' ability to get on with Joss much more easily than she could herself. He had opened up to them in a way he never had to her.

To her relief, she saw him glance at his watch and announce that it was time they were on their way.

Robert persuaded them to stay for a final coffee and liqueur, Joss refusing the liqueur since he was driving.

Nell recklessly allowed Robert to order a brandy for her, downing the fiery liquid in four nervous gulps. She didn't normally drink a great deal since she had a catastrophically weak head, something she had discovered in her teens. This evening, though, she felt she needed the numbing release of the powerful alcohol, and it certainly seemed to be having an effect, she acknowledged drowsily as they walked back to the Rolls.

'No, you get in the front with Joss,' Liz told her, pushing her gently towards the front passenger seat when she would have joined her friends in the back.

It was only a few minutes' drive from the restaurant to the house; Nell's shopping and suit-cases had already been stowed away in the boot, and, after having said their goodnights and arranged when Liz would arrive for the wedding, Joss turned the car in the direction of their journey home.

Neither of them spoke, Nell because she felt too drowsy, Joss, she suspected, because he had nothing to say to her. Why had he come to collect her himself? Had he really thought she might try to renege on their agreement?'

She would have had to return home some time. Sleepily she snuggled down in the seat, breathing in the rich scent of the leather, mingled with the warm maleness of Joss's skin. Her eyelashes fluttered softly as she fought against the waves of sleep and then gave in to them, a small, inarticulate sound half parting her lips as she subsided into sleep.

As she slept, she turned away from Joss, and, catching the movement out of the corner of his eye, he depressed the brake slightly and turned to look at her, his face grim and shadowed, and for the first time in recent weeks he questioned the validity of his own sanity. He was gambling more dangerously then he had ever gambled before. And why? Because . . .

He cursed as a car coming the other way cut the corner and blinded him with its headlights, dismissing his private thoughts in favour of concentrating on the heavy traffic. It was too late now to have doubts and second thoughts. Aim high, his teacher had told him. Aim as high as there is, and don't think about the consequences of falling.

Twice before in his life he had been lucky. Once in that teacher who had selflessly and generously given him his time and attention, teaching him, nurturing his intelligence until he was able to see for himself that there could be a life for him beyond the confines of that experienced by the rest of his family. Over the years he had treated them generously, tried to encourage them to reach out and grasp life's opportunities as he had done, but they did not share his ambition, and they were content to remain where they were, enjoying his generosity.

He felt alien to them now, and they to him. He saw them rarely, and when he did he sensed that they were uncomfortable with him.

Now that his grandparents were both dead there was nothing to take him back. He wondered what his grandfather would think if he could see him now. How many times had he prophesied that Joss would come to a bad end, as he wielded the leather strap he kept for chastising his male offspring. There had been no sadistic cruelty behind the blows; it was merely that his grandfather knew of no other way of disciplining an unruly child.

Not really wanting to pursue such a potentially uncomfortable train of thought, he switched his concentration to the future, and the faint but disturbing rumours which had come to his ears that there were potential problems with an American corporation he had invested heavily in. This gift he had for playing the stock and commodities markets was one he treated with respect.

He drove on into the night.

The Rolls purred to a halt outside Easterhay. Nell stirred briefly in her sleep, murmured something unintelligible and snuggled back against the leather.

Joss reached across to wake her and then changed his mind, instead unfastening his seat-belt and then hers, and then striding round to her side of the car to lift her bodily out of her seat.

Johnson had the door open before he reached it, and as he shook his head at the old man's look of consternation, he whispered, 'She's only asleep. I thought I wouldn't wake her. Which is her room?'

As he told him, Joss reflected that despite the fact that he probably paid his staff well over double what Nell paid hers he would never command the affection and concern from them which Nell's gave to her.

Of course, they had been with the family for a long time, and staff could be notoriously snobbish. Doubtless there was far more to be said to be working for Lady Eleanor then there was for plain Joss Wycliffe.

When he reached the top of the stairs, he was breathing harder then he had been originally, but Nell was hardly any weight at all. In fact, she was too thin. He frowned slightly. These last months had taken their toll on her, visibly so. Her bedroom door was open. He walked in, grimacing over its shabbiness and lack of heat.

The house had no central heating. A needless expense, her grandfather had called it. He flipped back the coverlet and placed her beneath it, pulling it round her still fully clad body.

And then, before quitting the room, he stood for several minutes looking down at her. Was he doing the right thing? For himself or for her?

Only time would tell.

Closing her door quietly, he set off for the stairs and then paused, turning back. He knew the layout of the house because her grandfather had once shown him round it. He walked down the corridor, and hesitated for a few seconds before finding the door he wanted.

It opened into a large room positioned at the corner of the house, so that its windows overlooked both the front and the side of the park. The air in the room tasted of dust and emptiness; the bed was stripped; the furniture unpolished. Off this room were a bathroom, a dressing-room and a small sitting-room.

It was the suite traditionally occupied by the master and mistress of the house.

Nell's grandfather had moved out of it when his wife had died and, by the looks of it, it had been empty ever since.

He tried to visualise himself sharing it with Nell and found, depressingly, that he could not. It was too late to turn back. He had promised her grand-father that he would look after her, and besides . . .

His mouth compressing, he walked out of the room and closed the door.

Downstairs, Johnson was waiting to let him out.

'I'll just bring in Nell's cases and parcels,' Joss told him. 'Tell Mrs Booth to let her sleep in in the morning,' he added brusquely. 'She's not had an easy time of it lately.'


Nell stared at the delicate face of the small travelling alarm Liz had given her as a twenty-first present in consternation. Ten o'clock! It couldn't be!

She got up and dressed quickly, dismayed by the state of her new clothes. She had no memory of arriving home or being put to bed, but she suspected it must have been Joss who had carried her there.

No wonder he had left her fully dressed.

She pulled a face at herself as she put on one of her old skirts and sweaters, shocked to discover how frumpish they were. Those few days in Cambridge had certainly opened her eyes. She longed to put on her new jeans and one of the bright tops, but they

Here are your BIG WIN Game Tickets, worth from $5.00 to $1,000,000.00 each. Scratch off the PINK METALLIC STRIP on each of your sweepstakes tickets to see what you could win and mail your entry right away. (See official rules in back of book for details!)

*This could be your lucky day - GOOD LUCK!*

**FOLD AND DETACH ALONG THIS DOTTED LINE—RETURN ALL GAME TICKETS INTACT.**

**TICKET 1**
Scratch PINK METALLIC STRIP to reveal potential value of this ticket if it is a winning ticket. Return all game tickets intact.

LUCKY NUMBER

5 1 3 8 1 7 3 9

**TICKET 2**
Scratch PINK METALLIC STRIP to reveal potential value of this ticket if it is a winning ticket. Return all game tickets intact.

LUCKY NUMBER

10 3 7 9 3 2 4

**TICKET 3**
Scratch PINK METALLIC STRIP to reveal potential value of this ticket if it is a winning ticket. Return all game tickets intact.

LUCKY NUMBER

2 1 3 7 8 9 7 5

**TICKET 4**
Scratch PINK METALLIC STRIP to reveal potential value of this ticket if it is a winning ticket. Return all game tickets intact.

LUCKY NUMBER

4 1 3 8 2 2 6 7

**TICKET 5**
We're giving away brand new books to selected individuals. Scratch PINK METALLIC STRIP for number of free books you will receive.

AUTHORIZATION CODE

130107-742

**TICKET 6**
We have an outstanding added gift for you if you are accepting our free books. Scratch PINK METALLIC STRIP to reveal gift.

AUTHORIZATION CODE

130107-742

**YES!** Enter my Lucky Numbers in The BIG WIN Sweepstakes and tell me if I've won any cash prize. If PINK METALLIC STRIP is scratched off on ticket #5, I will also receive one or more FREE Harlequin Presents® novels along with the FREE GIFT on ticket #6, as explained on the opposite page.    U-H-P-11/89 108 CIH CAPD

NAME _____

ADDRESS _____ APT. _____

CITY _____ STATE _____ ZIP _____

Offer limited to one per household and not valid to current Presents subscribers.
© 1989 HARLEQUIN ENTERPRISES LTD.

Printed in Canada

Carefully detach card along dotted lines and mail today! Play all your BIG WIN tickets and get everything you're entitled to—including FREE BOOKS and a FREE GIFT!

NO POSTAGE
NECESSARY
IF MAILED
IN THE
UNITED STATES

## BUSINESS REPLY MAIL
FIRST CLASS MAIL    PERMIT NO. 717    BUFFALO, NY

POSTAGE WILL BE PAID BY ADDRESSEE

## HARLEQUIN READER SERVICE
## THE BIG WIN SWEEPSTAKES

901 FUHRMANN BLVD
PO BOX 1867
BUFFALO NY 14240-9952

must still be in the boot of Joss's Rolls.

She went first to the kitchen, demanding crisply to know why she hadn't been woken at her normal time.

Mrs Booth looked flustered and, when pressed, confessed that it had been Joss who had given the order that she was to be allowed to sleep.

Compressing her lips, Nell refused her offer of breakfast. Was it silly of her to resent the fact that the staff were already paying more heed to Joss's commands than to hers?

Making herself a cup of coffee, she went into the library to check over the mail. While she was there, the phone rang, and a cool, feminine voice asked, 'May I speak to Lady Eleanor?'

'Speaking,' Nell told her.

'Ah . . . I've been asked to ring you by Mr Joss Wycliffe's secretary. She's commissioned me to draw up some schemes for the interior design of Easterhay, and I was wondering when I could come round to look over the house.'

Nell stared at the telephone in disbelief, too angry to speak. How dared Joss do this to her? She was perfectly capable of finding her own interior designer . . . In fact, she was perfectly capable of doing the work herself. She longed to simply tell the woman her services were not needed, but she had been brought up from childhood to be polite and deferential, no matter what her own private feelings, and so she said calmly, 'Not at the moment, I'm afraid. May I come back to you?'

When she did, it would be to tell her that her services were not required. She might be forced to marry Joss, she might be idiotic enough to love him, she might have allowed her friend, on his behalf, to revamp her wardrobe and her appearance, but she was not going to allow someone else to dictate to her how her home should be decorated and furnished, she decided wrathfully, completely overlooking the fact that she had been contemplating doing just that only a very short time ago. That had been different. Then the designer would have been chosen by her instead of inflicted on her by Fiona.

She had scarcely replaced the receiver when Johnson arrived to tell her that a Miss Howard had arrived.

Nell looked at him blankly.

'I believe she's Mr Joss's secretary,' he informed her.

Joss's secretary, here.

Before Nell could say a word, the elegant brunette was walking past Johnson and into the room.

She gave Nell a dismissive look from frosty blue eyes, one dark eyebrow lifting in elegant disdain as she surveyed the room.

'Joss said that the place was rather run-down. Just as well you're holding the reception in a marquee. That's what I've come to discuss with you, by the way. I've brought menus from several caterers. I expect you'll want to have the usual Sloaney-type thing,' she added contemptuously. 'Watercress soup, salmon, strawberries and cream . . .'

She said it as though she decision was hers and hers alone; the menu already a *fait accompli*, and a burning shaft of anger exploded inside Nell.

'You're a little out of date,' she told her coolly, refusing to give in to the intimidating frown turned on her, and added calmly, 'Thank you, Johnson, Perhaps you could ask Mrs Booth to provide us with coffee,' thus dismissing their interested audience.

'That would be perfectly acceptable for a late spring or early summer wedding,' she added, 'but not for the autumn. You must have been reading too many out-of-date copies of the *Tatler*. And as for holding the reception in a marquee, it will be held in the ballroom,' she announced, her head held high.

As the words left her lips, she was astounded at her own temerity. What on earth had happened to her? It was plain from her face that Joss's secretary was as stunned as she was herself. Dark colour streaked her elegantly made-up cheekbones, and she suddenly looked older and harder.

'Well, then,' she said brittly, 'what exactly do you suggest? Although I must warn you that Joss has extremely demanding standards. The business associates he's inviting to this wedding will expect to be properly entertained.'

Nell was furious, but she controlled her anger this time. How dared Joss allow his secretary to come here and attempt to browbeat her like this? Their wedding might be a business arrangement, but it was still first and foremost a wedding, not a business meeting, and as such was not going to be masterminded by Joss's secretary.

'I think the wedding breakfast menu is something you can safely leave to me,' she said calmly. 'And now, if you'll excuse me . . .'

'Joss has sent me down here for the whole day. He said you would need help getting organised. I'll have to tell him, of course, that you've rejected my advice. He won't be pleased. As I've already said, he sets very high standards, and since it's his money that's paying . . .'

She stopped and smiled thinly.

'Is that what he told you?' Nell enquired lightly, not letting her real feelings show. She saw a faint shadow of something darken the other woman's eyes, and guessed that she had merely assumed that Joss would be paying. It gave her the courage to continue quietly, 'Actually, he's not. Not that it's any concern of yours. As to your assisting me . . . I really don't think that's necessary or desirable.'

She sat down in the same dismissive manner she remembered her headmistress using to good effect. 'I'm sorry you've had a wasted journey over here.'

She was still shaking half an hour after her unwanted visitor had left.

It was an hour after that that Joss walked into the library unannounced, his face dark with anger.

Although inside she was terrified, Nell managed to keep her face calm.

'Why did you send Fiona back?' he demanded without preamble.

'Because I don't need her,' Nell told him bravely. 'I'm perfectly capable of organising our wedding myself, Joss. I might have no option but to agree to this marriage, but I will not be bullied and told what to do by your secretary.'

'She's extremely efficient and experienced.'

'I don't doubt it,' Nell murmured with a touch of cynicism that made his eyes harden.

'Just what are you trying to imply?' he demanded harshly.

'Nothing,' Nell returned promptly. 'Had you asked me first if I wanted your secretary's assistance, I would have told you that I didn't. Just as I would also have told you that I am perfectly capable of finding my own interior designer if need be.

'This wedding may be a business arrangement
. . . and I may be very much the junior partner, but
I will not be dictated to by your secretary, Joss, nor
by anyone else.' She saw him frown, and felt her
temper ease from her; sighing slightly, she said,
'Joss, if you have so little faith in my ability and so
much in your secretary's, perhaps you should be
marrying her . . . but then of course she can't
provide your son with a foothold in the peerage, can
she? I appreciate that it's no concern of mine what
role she plays in your life, but I won't have her
interfering in mine . . . whatever her relationship
with you.'

It was as close as she dared to go in telling him
that she suspected that he and his secretary were or
had been lovers. She had suspected it from the
moment she met the other woman. There had been a
certain mocking challenge in those too calculating
blue eyes; a certain arrogant determination to let
Nell know that she considered her position very
much inferior to her own; and from her attitude Nell
had come to the conclusion that she was far more to
Joss than merely his secretary.

'Whatever . . .' His mouth snapped shut and he
glared at her. 'Fiona is my secretary and nothing
else, but, as you say,' he added cruelly, 'my
relationship with her has nothing to do with you.
Jealous of her, Nell?'

She was shaking inside, but determined to hold
herself together and not betray what she was feeling.

She deliberately chose to misunderstand him and
to use the weapon she knew to be most lethal.

'Jealous? Of someone who doesn't know that one
never serves a summer menu once the game season
starts?' She allowed her eyebrow to lift slightly,

and said indifferently, 'Hardly.'

'No . . . she isn't of your class, Nell, and there's really no need to underline that fact. But then, neither am I, and when I bring my secretary to this house, I shall expect her to be treated with respect.'

Nell turned to look at him. 'Respect has to be earned, Joss. It can't be commanded . . . nor bought. Did you want to discuss anything else with me?' she added carelessly, when the silence had stretched for too long. Joss was looking at her almost as though he hated her. Perhaps he did, she thought wildly.

'No,' he told her harshly; and before she could say another word he had left.

# CHAPTER SIX

WITH less than a month to go before the wedding, Nell was determined to prove to Joss that her powers of organisation were equal to the combined efforts of his secretary and his interior designers, even though she might exhaust herself in the process.

Perhaps it was as well if she did. It would leave her less time to think, to dwell on the enormity of what she was going to do.

A curt phone call from Joss had reminded her that he expected that they would both inhabit the master suite of the house from the day of their marriage, and, with the ideas and information garnered from Liz, Nell called Mrs Booth into the library for a conference of what could and could not be achieved.

Between them, the existing staff, who had learned to turn their hands to almost anything and everything during the years they had worked for her grandfather, confirmed that they could tackle all the renovations and redecoration Nell had in mind.

She had worked long into the night for the three days since her return from Cambridge, drawing up lists and making plans.

Telephone calls to suppliers in London had taken care of the ordering of the wallpapers and fabrics she would need, and Mrs Knowles in the village had confirmed that she and her daughter and niece together could just about make up the fabric Nell had ordered in time for the wedding.

The sketches and photographs culled from

magazines that Nell showed her had made her marvel a little, but she was a skilled needlewoman with enough confidence in her own ability to boost Nell's flagging spirits. After three days of non-stop endeavour, she was beginning to wonder if she should after all have simply given in and allowed Joss to organise everything.

But if she gave in now, what would her life with him be like? If she did produce a son, he would probably have the child taken away from her, insisting on having him brought up by nannies and other hired, qualified staff, and Nell was not going to have that.

In fact, Nell was discovering a fighting spirit she had never even guessed she possessed. It disturbed her to realise how very protective she felt already of a child she had not yet even conceived.

She even found herself walking the length of the long gallery when she ought to have been doing other things, studying the features in the family portraits, wondering whether her child would take after her family or look like his father.

Her child . . . She shivered a little. The child would not merely be hers, but Joss's as well, and he would have his own definite ideas about his upbringing.

At times when she ought to have been concentrating on wallpapers and fabrics, she found herself dreamily wondering, picturing a baby with Joss's dark features, a child whom she could love as much because he was cast in his father's image as for himself, and then she caught herself up sharply. Their child would be an individual, not a mirror-image of his father. He would have his own traits and characteristics, his own very definite personality.

Within four days of her return home, she had marshalled her workforce, and on Wednesday morning they began stripping the wallpaper from the master bedroom and preparing it for redecorating.

She was on her mettle now, and determined to prove to Joss that she could revamp the house as well as his interior designer.

Something in her, in fact, was actually enjoying the challenge. The money she had been so carefully hoarding against her uncertain future could now be spent in the knowledge that the sale of the dinner-service would replenish her bank account and more than cover the cost of the wedding.

While her team of decorators worked upstairs, down in the kitchen Mrs Booth was organising the arrangements for the wedding breakfast.

She and Nell had pored over recipe books inherited from Nell's great-great-grandmother in an attempt to find something not just suitable but different enough to surprise Joss's friends.

Perhaps it was unworthy of her to want to do this, but Nell reflected that everyone was allowed a little bit of ego-boosting every now and again.

By Friday the master suite was ready for its new raiment; the walls stripped of their dusty paper and dull hangings, the woodwork of its old-fashioned, dark brown varnish. It was amazing how light and airy the room looked, Nell reflected, studying it. Down in the village, Mrs Knowles and her helpers were already working on the new hangings for the bed; she had chosen a soft peach fabric with a design on it in French blue. The walls were to be papered in a companion paper in a trellis design above the dado rail, and sponged in toning peach below it. A border that exactly matched the fabric just above the dado rail would complete the redecoration, and she had decided to continue the same colour theme throughout the entire suite.

Luckily her grandfather had never replaced the old Edwardian white sanitaryware, now back in fashion. The bathroom was a good size and the estate carpenter was making a matching dado rail for both the bathroom and the dressing-room.

In the sitting-room, she was using a slightly more formal companion paper, and here the curtains were to be plain peach lined with a subtly patterned fabric in shadow stripes.

Mrs Knowles had promised that all the curtains, chair and settee covers, cushions and bed hangings would be finished on time, and Nell knew that she could rely on her.

Walking round the bare rooms, the furniture pushed into the middle of them and covered in dusty covers, she tried to visualise how they were going to look, praying that she had not made any errors.

It was too late now for cold feet, she told herself, leaving the men to their work and going back downstairs.

Out of the downstairs room only two needed a minimum of work, one being the library and the other the dining-room, its red Chinese silk wallcovering being, in her opinon, too beautiful to destroy.

Some of the rooms would have to remain untouched for now, but if she could just prove to Joss that she was fully capable of organising the work herself they could be tackled later.

She wandered into the drawing-room, wondering what he would think of the colour scheme she had chosen for the large south-facing room.

She was hoping that the subtle mixture of blues and terracottas; the faded elegance of the pieces of antique furniture she had decided should furnish the room, would meet with his approval.

On Friday she was on tenterhooks, wondering if Joss would come round to see her, but he rang late in the afternoon, his voice cool and impersonal, to announce that he would be out of the country for ten days on business.

She gave a faint sigh of relief, and then wondered sadly how many brides would have shared her relief at hearing such news.

Very few

On Saturday, Grania arrived unexpectedly, a man Nell had not seen before in tow.

Nell had reminded her about the marriage over the telephone, and, apart from saying derisively that she could not imagine why on earth Joss would want to marry her, she had made no comment.

Nell wasn't entirely surprised now to hear that Grania had changed her mind about being a bridesmaid.

'In fact, darling, I might not be able to make it at all,' she added airily. 'Guy and I could well be in Sardinia . . .'

Nell made no comment, although she could see that her stepsister's companion looked a little embarrassed.

Grania didn't stay long, seeking Nell out privately to ask her for a small loan.

When Nell discovered that her idea of a small loan was several thousand pounds, she was stunned, and had to refuse.

'Oh, come on, darling. You can easily afford it now. Don't tell me Joss isn't paying very handsomely indeed to join the family.'

How many other people had come to the same conclusion? Nell wondered miserably, when Grania had gone, leaving the house in a temper when she discovered that Nell wasn't prepared to advance her the money.

Everyone locally knew her position; would they, like Grania, immediately leap to the conclusion that the only reason Joss could be marrying her was because she had something he wanted, and he could afford to pay for it? It was one thing to have to acknowledge to herself the basis on which their marriage was formed; it was another to suspect that others knew it as well, even thought she suspected she was being naïve in hoping they might have accepted that it was a love match.

Who, looking at her, would ever think that Joss was in love with her? Oh, her new clothes, her new self-confidence, had improved her appearance, but nothing could elevate it to match that of the women Joss favoured.

Grania's acid comment denigrated them both.

She spent the rest of the day writing out wedding invitations, walking down to the village to post them early in the evening, taking the short cut through the park.

The scent of autumn crisped the air, the trees stark against the horizon without their softening leaves.

A group of women chatting outside the post office turned to look at her. Nell knew them, normally would not have given their interest in her a second thought. Today though, her sensitivities rasped by what Grania had said to her, she found herself instinctively tucking her left hand out of sight, and hurrying past them with only the briefest acknowledgement.

The weekend brought no contact from Joss, several telephone calls from people who had already received their invitations, including Nell's godmother, whose husband was Lord Lieutentant of the county. They

chatted for a while, Lady Worboys wanting to know all
the details of their engagement.

She had met Joss once, briefly, at a small Christmas
party held by Nell's grandfather the year before he
died.

'I suspected then that he was rather interested in
you. I'm so glad you're not having a long engagement,
darling. They're never a good idea. Now . . . is there
anything I can do to help?' she asked practically.

Nell thanked her and said no. She loved her godmother, but she was rather inclined to view life
through rose-coloured glasses, and Nell was feeling far
too sensitive to endure her well-meaning but painful
chatter above love and happy-ever-afters.

She was just on the point of going to bed when the
telephone rang again. She picked it up listlessly, almost
dropping it when she heard Joss's vigorous voice
demanding, 'Nell, is that you?'

'Joss!' she exclaimed faintly. 'When did you get
home? I thought you were in America.'

'I am,' he told her drily, adding, 'They do have tele-
phones over here, you know, Nell. How are things
progressing?'

Instantly the happiness that followed her shock was
destroyed by a bitter awareness that the only reason he
had rung was to check up on her. He was probably
worried that her standards of organisation wouldn't
match up to those of his secretary, she thought wrathfully.

'Very well,' she told him crisply, matching the busi-
nesslike tone of her voice to his. 'I've sent out all the
invitations. Several people have rung this weekend to
accept. Joss . . .' A thought that had been niggling at
the back of her mind all week put to flight her chagrin.
'I noticed you hadn't included any members of your

family on your list . . .'

'I've already told you, Nell,' he interrupted her harshly, 'my family go their way and I go mine. Even if I invited them, they wouldn't want to come. They wouldn't feel comfortable, you see, hobnobbing wi' such grand folk,' he mimicked the Glaswegian accent of his youth, and beneath the harsh words Nell sensed a frisson of pain.

'You've not changed your mind about marrying me, then?'

The curt words surprised her.

'Did you expect me to?' she asked unevenly when she recovered from her shock.

'Hardly.'

If she closed her eyes she could actually visualise the cynical twist of his mouth, its well-cut upper lip curling slightly.

'It's isn't in the de Tressail make-up, is it, to go back on their given word, and besides, you can't afford not to marry me, can you, Nell?'

Surely that couldn't be bitterness she could hear underlying the drawled words? Surely it couldn't be that Joss . . . hard, unfeeling, unemotional Joss was suffering from the same stinging self-awareness of what others might read into their marriage as she was herself?

She closed her eyes and took a deep breath, and then, before she could lose her courage, she said huskily, 'Joss, are you on your own?'

There was a brief pause, during which she could almost feel his surprise at her question.

'Yes,' he said curtly. 'Why?'

'When . . . when we get married, I'd like everyone else to believe that it's . . . that it's because we . . . we care about one another. I . . . I think it would be better for both of us if they did . . .' She was stumbling over the words now, her tension increased by his complete lack of response. The empty silence between them almost hummed. What was he thinking? What was he going to say? Would he reject her request? Would he demand to know why she had made it. Or would he understand?

'A love-match . . . between you and me? Do you really think the world will be so easily deceived, Nell?'

She had to stifle her sharp cry of distress. Perhaps he was right to remind her that no one, other than perhaps her godmother, was likely to believe for one minute that Joss Wycliffe could possibly have fallen in love with plain Nell de Tressail, but surely, just this once, he could have indulged her . . . humoured her . . . offered her a sop to her pride and pretended that they might get away with it?

'No . . . No, I don't suppose they would,' she agreed stiffly, her voice dull.

As she replaced the receiver she heard him call out sharply, 'Nell . . . Nell . . .'

But she refused to respond, or to answer the telephone when it shrilled imperatively five minutes later.

She was behaving emotionally, idiotically, given the circumstances of their engagement and forthcoming marriage, but surely for once in her life she was entitled to throw aside her great-aunt's teaching and respond to her own inner emotions.

She slept badly and woke up with a pounding head, exacerbated by the smell of paint which was slowly permeating the house.

Her mood, a combination of dread, pain and irritation, seemed to have afflicted the rest of the household as well as herself.

'Wedding nerves,' Liz told her philosophically when she telephoned her later in the day. 'How are things going apart from that?'

'Not too bad,' Nell told her. 'The master bedroom is nearly finished. Mrs Knowles is bringing the new curtains today and the carpets should be back by the end of the week.'

Thanks to Liz she had found a concern in London that specialised in cleaning antique rugs and carpets.

'Is everything all right, Nell?' Liz interjected quietly. 'You sound very tense.'

'I'm fine,' she lied brittly.

But she wasn't and she suspected they both knew it. How on earth was she going to cope with the reality of being married to Joss when merely the thought of it was enough to have this kind of effect on her?

'It isn't too late to change your mind, you know,' Liz told her slowly.

Nell bit her lip. Change her mind . . . how could she? And yet, for one wild, panicky moment, she was sorely tempted. It was too much . . . *Joss* was too much but then sanity reasserted itself and she said huskily, 'Liz, I can't. I've given Joss my word, and besides, there's the house.'

'Nell, Nell . . . for once in your life put yourself first. And as for the house, Robert was saying only the other night that you could probably raise a bank loan on the security of it to pay off the death-duties . . . Nell, I'm so worried about you. Feeling the way you do about Joss, marriage to him will be hell for you . . .'

'Yes,' she acknowledged sadly, but, as she had told Liz, it was too late for her to change her mind. Too many arrangements had been made . . . too many things set in train. And then there was Joss himself. He would never forgive her if she humiliated him by

ending their engagement now. He would never understand that she had done it because she loved him.

'Mrs Knowles, they look marvellous,' Nell praised as
both she and the seamstress stood back to admire the
newly hung curtains.

Mrs Knowles had been as good as her word, and
she and her girls had arrived after lunch to hang the
new curtains up at the master bedroom windows.

The rich colours glowed against the newly decorated
walls, highlighting the delicate colour Nell had chosen
for them.

From all over the house, Nell had culled the best of
the most suitable antique furniture for the suite of
rooms. A pretty inlaid bureau, which had been a
favourite of her grandmother's, stood against one wall,
a heavy chest of drawers against another. The bed
itself had been polished until it shone, and a new
mattress ordered to replace the ancient, bumpy one
which Nell guessed must have been at least forty years
old. Now the mattress was obscured by the fabric
heaped upon it. Not only had Mrs Knowles completed
the curtains as she had promised, but the eiderdown,
bedspread, pillow-shams and chair-slips were also
ready.

'We should have the sofa-covers done by the middle
of the week, as well as the curtains for the sitting-room,
but I thought we'd better see how these looked up
first.'

'They look wonderful,' Nell told her truthfully, glad
now that she had followed her advice and bought the
extra yardage of fabric to allow for extra width, as she
saw how beautifully the curtains draped.

She remained in the room long after everyone else
had left.

The estate workers had almost finished decorating the downstairs rooms, and the silence that followed their departure was almost eerie. Nell had grown used to the bustle and noise of having them around, and now she remembered how lonely the house had often seemed to her as a child. She must make sure that her child never felt like that. This house needed more than one small baby to fill it. It needed a family.

Of its own accord, her heart fluttered shallowly in her breast, her stomach muscles cramping.

A family . . . yes, that was what she craved more than anything else: the sense of belonging that came from being part of an enclosed family unit; the pleasure of giving and receiving love.

'Nell?'

She tensed as she heard Joss's voice outside the bedroom door.

Joss was in America . . . What was he doing here? Confused and nervous, one hand crept to her throat as she stood up and stared at the door.

She saw him frown and check as he walked in, saying abruptly, 'Mrs Booth said you were up here . . .'

While his attention was on the room and not on her, she had the chance to compose herself, to control the soft responsiveness of her body and the eager warmth in her eyes.

'Yes . . . we've just finished hanging the curtains.'

He looked at her then, his frown deepening.

'*We?*' he queried. 'Mrs Booth told me that you'd been up here on your own for nearly an hour. From the way she said it, I suspect she imagines you were indulging in some sort of romantic bridal fantasy.'

Nell had to turn away to hide the stain of colour surging into her face.

'Has it really been an hour?' she said unsteadily. 'I had no idea. I'd better go down.'

She started to walk past him, and then tensed as he reached out and stopped her, catching hold of her wrist with his fingers. She saw him look down at her clenched hand.

'Nervous, Nell?'

Something in the way he looked at her made the nerves flutter under her skin.

'Just a little tense, that's all,' she fibbed, adding desperately when he refused to let her look away from him, 'There's been a lot to do.'

With her free hand she indicated their surroundings, and to her relief he looked away from her and said calmly, 'Yes. You've done very well in here.' He looked at the bed and added quietly, 'I trust you realise that we shall be sharing this room, Nell.'

She couldn't help it. A wild surge of colour flooded her skin and she looked desperately away from Joss himself, trying to focus on something—*anything* that meant she did not have to look at him.

She heard him laugh, a soft, very male sound that sent tiny frissons of sensation coursing over her skin, and into the silence that followed she poured a torrent of husky, nervous words in a voice so unlike her normal one that she barely recognised it herself.

'I didn't think you'd be back so soon . . . What was the flight like? You must be tired. When did you get back?'

'I came back ahead of schedule, the flight was fine. Yes, I am a little tired,' Joss responded imperturbably, before cutting across another spate of nervous questions by saying quietly, 'Nell, I've been thinking. You're right. It would be better for both our sakes, as you said, if we allowed the rest of the world to believe that this is a love-match.'

She focused on him then, too stunned to do anything else. She had expected that that tiny, betraying plea of hers would never be referred to again, and to have Joss bring it up and, what was more, approve of it, made her forget her embarrassment.

'There is just one thing, though,' he added almost musingly. His fingers were still circling her wrist, and now subtly their pressure increased, and became almost caressing as they found the place where her pulse beat frantically against her blue-veined skin. 'At the moment I doubt we'd be able to convince anyone that we're in love. Lovers carry with them an aura of intimacy that's very easy to discern. Lovers touch and kiss.'

Imperceptibly he had drawn her closer to him, and Nell trembled as she felt the heat and power of his body against her own.

She opened her mouth to protest, saying his name with a quick, husky breath.

'It's all right, Nell. I'm only going to kiss you. We want to convince the world that we're in love, remember.'

He touched her mouth with his own, a light, caressing movement of warm flesh against flesh which demanded nothing but which still made her tremble wildly as she fought the aching need inside her to throw caution aside and kiss him back.

His mouth left hers, and slowly caressed the soft skin of her throat.

'Nell.' How husky his voice sounded against her ear, almost as though he was as affected by caressing her as she was by his touch. 'We want to convince the world that we're in love—remember? When I kiss you, open your mouth.'

His lips were so close to her ear, she could feel their touch. The warmth of his breath made her shiver, tiny waves of sensation tingling through her body.

'Joss,' she protested weakly, 'I ought to go down-stairs. Mrs Booth will wonder . . .'

'If we're making love?'

Her face burned. That wasn't what she had intended to say at all. Joss saw the shock in her eyes and his mouth curled cynically.

'How illuminating those eyes of yours are, Nell. I wonder how I'm going to like being married to a woman who can't quite hide her distaste of me.'

His accusation stunned her. Incautiously she responded immediately, 'Joss, that isn't true.'

'Isn't it? Then kiss me properly, Nell. Not like a little girl obliged to kiss a much disliked relative.'

His head bent towards her and she quivered tensely, closing her eyes. She felt the warmth of his breath against her lips and tremulously allowed them to part, waiting for the warm pressure of his mouth against her own, willing herself not to make a complete fool of herself and responded wildly to it. But nothing happened.

Her eyelids fluttered and opened. Joss was watching her, the golden eyes gleaming fire.

'No, Nell,' he said softly. 'This time, you kiss me.'

Her shock showed in her face.

'Poor Nell . . . There's no need to look so terrified.'

His taunt stung, and before she could think properly she flung tartly at him, 'I suppose the next thing you'll be telling me is that you don't bite.'

She saw his face change, his expression suddenly predatory and alien.

'Ah, but I do.'

Something in her face must have given her away,
because she saw his eyes darken and blaze.

'Shall I show you, Nell?' he demanded thickly. 'Is
that what you want? Underneath that cool, icy disdain
do you really ache, just like the rest of us? Shall I find
out?'

She was shivering, but not from fear or cold.

And then his mouth was on hers. Not gently or
lightly, but hotly, demandingly, his tongue probing the
parted outline of her lips and tasting the sweetness
within.

All her senses came alive at once, her body singing
with pleasure, her decision never to allow him to see
how he affected her swept away as though it had never
been.

Her hands gripped his shoulders, smoothing their
powerful breadth as they slid beneath his jacket; she
felt him tense and then gather her in against his body
so that she was aware of its physical arousal.

The knowledge both surprised and thrilled her.

'Ah, Joss . . . there you are.'

The cool, female voice tore into her fragile fantasy
and, although it was Nell who pulled back first at the
sound of Fiona Howard's voice, it was Joss who
regained control first, his body apparently fully under
control, while hers shivered and ached.

'You said there were some letters you wanted to get
off tonight, so I thought I'd better come and find you.
There's that reception this evening as well . . .'

She was speaking to Joss but she was looking at
Nell, her eyes hardening as she looked deliberately at
the swollen fullness of her mouth.

There was no apology for interrupting them, Nell
noticed angrily; no question of her right to invade their
privacy . . . no doubt in her mind about which of them

held the most power . . . the most influence, and
Nell recognised that in refusing to allow her to
mastermind the wedding . . . in snubbing her, she
had made herself a bitter enemy.

But they would have been enemies anyway. Yes,
but she could have been more subtle . . . could have
hidden her own jealousy, she acknowledged wryly.
Now, as Fiona continued her unsubtle scrutiny, she
tilted her chin proudly, her eyes cool as she stepped
past her and said distantly to Joss, 'I'd better go
down. I promised I'd go over the menu with Mrs
Booth.'

'I see you've had interior designers in, after all,'
Fiona commented as she and Joss fell into step
beside her. Fiona was standing much closer to Joss
than she was, Nell noticed miserably, but she
allowed no trace of what she was feeling to show in
her face.

She had already betrayed herself enough for one
day. She just hoped that Joss would put her response
down to pure sexual arousal and not guess at her real
feelings. The fact that he had been aroused himself
might incline him to such a conclusion.

The speed of his arousal had been something
which had surprised her. Surely a man of his
experience . . . Or perhaps he had *wanted* her to
believe that he desired her. Perhaps he had even
deliberately manufactured a physical response to
her. The thought made her feel faintly sick, and she
didn't bother responding to Fiona's taunt.

Joss did, however, turning to his secretary and
saying calmly, 'You're wrong, Fiona. Nell
organised all this herself. It seems my fiancée has
hidden talents.' He turned to look at her and Nell
felt her whole body go hot under the sensual

inspection of his scrutiny.

Fiona was obviously aware of it too, because, when Joss excused himself to collect some papers he had left in the library, she turned to Nell and hissed acidly, 'I hope you're not going to be stupid enough to fall in love with him. The last thing Joss wants hanging around his neck is a doting little wife.'

Angry and unnerved by the extent of her physical response to him, Nell responded sharply, 'Fall in love with Joss? Oh, I don't think so.'

And then she turned on her heel and prepared to leave, only to stop as she saw Joss himself standing just inside the door.

There was no doubt that he must have heard her. His mouth was compressed into a thin, angry line. For a moment she was tempted to go to him and explain, but she stopped herself. She wasn't going to say anything while Fiona was there, watching gloatingly.

But why was he so angry? She knew they had agreed that they would at least attempt to pretend that their marriage was based on love, but his secretary was hardly like to be deceived, especially not since she and Joss had been, and probably still were, lovers.

Tensing her body proudly, she walked past him, saying coolly, 'Since you've so much work to do, Joss, I'd better not keep you.'

It was only her early training instilled into her by her great-aunt that prevented her from going upstairs and shutting herself away in her room.

Instead, she very pointedly escorted them both to the front door and then, when they had gone, she went upstairs to her room and sat and stared at her wedding dress in its dustproof covering, and wondered how on earth she was going to get through the rest of her life.

# CHAPTER SEVEN

AFTER Joss had gone, the day suddenly seemed flat, despite the fact that she had not been anticipating seeing him. She wondered what had made him cut short his business trip, and then admitted to herself that she was scarcely likely to find out.

When he had initially proposed to her, she had harboured in some deep recess of her imagination the illusion that, even if he could never come to love her, they could develop a deep and enduring friendship; she had allowed herself to daydream of quiet, intimate evenings when he would unburden himself to her and discuss with her the problems of his business life. Now she recognised how idiotic she had been. Joss had no need of her to unburden himself to; if fact, he should want to do something so out of character, anyway, he had his faithful secretary.

Nell's mouth tightened. She had as good as made a rod for her own back by announcing to him that his relationship with Fiona was not her concern. Now she regretted those hasty words. How on earth could he even pretend to want to create an illusion that they were marrying for love, when he was having an affair with someone else?

That kiss . . . that passion . . . had they been for her?

She felt physically sick and got up unsteadily. In less than a fortnight this familiar room she had slept in since childhood would no longer be hers. Instead she would be sharing the master suite with Joss. Sleeping next to him in the huge old bed that had been in the family since the days of Charles II.

She would not be the first female member of her family to enter a loveless marriage—far from it, and even these days, in moneyed and powerful circles, marriage were often still very much parentally instituted and approved, no matter how much this might be glossed over. So why did her heart rebel against what she knew was an eminently sensible course; why did she so wish that she could simply walk away?

If she was plain Nell Smith and not Lady Eleanor de Tressail, with no particular family pedigree, no title, no history stretching back over the decades, nothing to offer Joss other than herself, would he then want to marry her?

She knew the answer, and, more gallingly, she suspected everyone else would know it as well.

For her pride's sake, she ought to tell him that the wedding was off, but even as the thought formed she knew she wouldn't. She loved him too much. That knowledge terrified her. How could she even think of putting herself through what she was going to have to endure as his wife?

Oh, he would never be publicly or deliberately hurtful to her; he wasn't that kind of man. No, her pain would all be of her own making; it would come from knowing that, when he made love to her, it was out of duty . . . out of his need for her to conceive. That when he pretended to care for her, it was because he wanted others to believe it. There had been no pretence when he proposed to her; no attempt to persuade her that he might genuinely care for her as a person.

If he had, would she have believed him? Her heart gave a tiny jerk at the thought of Joss playing the would-be lover. She might not have been able to believe him, but she would have allowed herself to seem as though she did. Possibly. Where was her pride? Where was her backbone?

Work . . . work was the only panacea, and there was plenty of that still to be done.

Her appetite, never large at the best of times, seemed to have completely deserted her, and she laboured over the evening meal Mrs Booth had provided in the solitary chill of the small dining-room.

This was a room off the cold, panelled ladies' withdrawing-room, and as she studied its dull walls Nell tried to imagine how she might best brighten it up.

So far she had simply concentrated on those rooms she knew they would need to use.

Her grandfather had never approved of a heated dining-room and so there was not even a basic electric heater. After toying with her dinner, she reloaded the tray Mrs Booth had left and took it back to the kitchen.

The kitchen was as old-fashioned as the rest of the house, although Mrs Booth claimed that she preferred the Aga cooker now that she had grown used to it.

It was her evening off and Nell washed her own china and cutlery, drying them methodically and putting them away. A dishwashing machine would be a necessity if Joss planned to entertain, and they could do with a new freezer. The existing one had been bought second-hand, when Nell had deemed it a necessity so that they could store some of the fruit and vegetables produced in abundance by the kitchen garden.

The kitchen did not have units, but huge oak dressers built into the walls which housed the family china and glassware. Provisions were stored in the pantry, on shelves which ran all round the walls.

If she went into it, Nell knew she would find bottles of preserve and fruit from her great-aunt's day, all neatly labelled and dated. Although she and Mrs Booth still made jam and marmalade, the freezer had proved a boon when it came to preserving their fruit.

The stone-slabbed floor felt chilly when she stepped off the rug, and she shivered a little. If there was enough money left over from the sale of the dinner-service, she would find out about a more practical and warm floor-covering for the kitchen. Mrs Booth wasn't getting any younger, and it was unfair to expect her to put up with such uncomfortable conditions.

No doubt Joss's designer would have taken one look at the kitchen and condemned the whole thing. Just for a moment Nell allowed herself to dream of a light, airy kitchen with pretty units and labour-saving devices; and the kind of kitchen that was large enough to have a table in it . . . the kind of kitchen where she could work, and at the same time keep an eye on their children.

All the muscles in her stomach tensed. Joss's children . . . Her body pulsed and ached as though already it longed for them. She must not make the mistake of smothering them with the love she could not give Joss. She must allow them to be free. She could see so many pitfalls in the years ahead . . . If they had sons, would Joss want to send them to her

grandfather's old school, or would he agree with her
that boarding-school was not always the best
environment for children?

The pulsing ache turned to panic. There were so
many things they hadn't discussed . . . so much
about him she didn't know. She had no idea even
what he liked to eat, only how he liked his coffee.
What papers did he read? The *Financial Times*, no
doubt . . .

Vague, confusing thoughts whirled through her
mind.

She heard the doorbell ring and went to answer it.
Joss was standing outside. He frowned down at her,
and she bit her lip, realising she was still wearing the
same old clothes he had seen her in earlier.

He, in contrast, had changed, and as he stepped
inside she saw that he was wearing a leather blouson
jacket in a dark jade colour, the leather so soft-
looking that she almost reached out and touched it.

He brought in with him the scent of woodsmoke
and autumn, and when she frowned, looking into
the courtyard for his car, he said wryly, 'I walked.
After the transatlantic flight I felt I needed the
exercise.'

As he stood towering over her, all her doubts and
fears coalesced, and without even knowing she was
going to do so she heard herself saying huskily, 'I
can't marry you, Joss. It won't work. I don't know
the first thing about the way you live your life. I'm
not like your secretary, I . . .'

'Nell.'

The harsh warning note in his voice silenced her.
His mouth grim, he looked up and down the hall.

'What's the matter with you? You're practically
hysterical. Besides, this isn't something we can

discuss here, where we could be overheard.'

She walked towards the library door, but he stopped her.

'No, not there. Is our sitting-room finished yet?'

'*Our* sitting-room?' She looked at him.

'The one off the master bedroom.'

'Oh, no. Not quite.'

'Never mind. We'll go up there anyway. We're not likely to be disturbed there.'

The look he gave her made her skin flush.

'It wasn't my fault we were interrupted this afternoon. She's your secretary.' And much, much more, her voice implied, but she held the words back.

'Fiona hasn't accustomed herself to the fact that I'm going to be a married man yet,' he said smoothly. 'Is that why you can't marry me? Because of Fiona?' he asked her. 'Or is it because of Williams?'

They were at the top of the stairs and Nell tensed, but refused to look at him. 'This has nothing to do with David. Naturally I'm not too happy about the obviousness of your relationship with Fiona,' she agreed coolly, 'but no, that it isn't the reason. The reason is the one I gave you. We don't know enough about one another.'

They had reached the master suite. Joss opened the door and stepped back, forcing her to precede him.

As he closed the door, he said calmly, 'What is it you want to know?'

'Oh, Joss, it isn't like that. You must know what I mean,' she protested huskily.

But he wouldn't let her continue, interrupting her harshly to say, 'What I know is that in ten days' time you and I are going to be married. No one welches on a deal with me, Nell,' he told her curtly, 'and that includes you. I'm sorry if you're suffering from an attack of virginal timidity!' He saw her face and laughed sourly. 'Oh, come on, Nell. You didn't think I wouldn't know, did you? I promise you, if it's any comfort to you, that I could take you to bed here and now and within a very short space of time indeed make you forget what the very word doubt means, in spite of Williams.'

His voice had dropped to a husky, almost mesmerising tone that made the blood pulse hotly through her veins and her heartbeat increase into frantic little thuds that robbed her of breath and made her tremble slightly.

'Don't think I don't know what all this is about.' He looked at her mouth, and to her embarrassment Nell found her lips were parting softly. 'I could spend the next ten days telling you that there's nothing to be worried about . . . that I'm not a monster . . . that I've no intention of hurting you or frightening you, but I really think it would be much easier to banish all those doubts of yours if I just showed you.'

When he had come so close to her, Nell looked up at him and felt her world lurch and spin wildly out of control as she saw the dark glitter of his eyes: tawny-gold, predatory, the eyes of a male animal hunting its prey.

'You and I *will* be married, Nell,' he told her, his voice little more than a whisper against her ear, but the words reverberated into her heart. 'Did I frighten you this afternoon? I didn't mean to.'

And his lips caressed the soft shell of her ear, sending shock shivers racing through her.

'I haven't forgotten how little you know about the male animal.'

His mockery shocked her back to reality. She attempted to pull away from him and said huskily 'I'm twenty-four, Joss. Hardly a child.'

'But not yet truly a woman,' he suggested delicately, and her defiance fled.

She wanted to protest that there was more to being a woman than mere sexual experience, but the words formed a choking ball in her throat, as though she herself, in some deep secret place, feared that she was somehow less of an adult because of her sexual inexperience.

'Perhaps that's what's actually bothering you,' he suggested with a tiny smile. 'Not so much bridal nerves as bridal impatience, eh, Nell?'

She froze and glared at him. 'So, first I'm frigid and then I'm sex-starved. Well, it may interest you to know, Joss, that when I said I couldn't marry you because I knew nothing about you, sex was the very last thing on my mind.'

It wasn't quite the truth, but she was angry enough to ignore the tiny flutters of her conscience.

'After all . . . if I really want to know what you're like in bed, it wouldn't be very hard to find out, would it?' she added scornfully, knowing she was flirting with danger, but too angry to care. 'I'm sure your secretary, for instance, would be able to furnish me with a first-hand account of . . .'

She gasped as he grabbed and shook her.

'Why, you little . . . Fiona is not and never has been my lover,' he told her acidly.

'That's not what you said before,' Nell challenged him, and nor was it what Fiona's whole demeanour had told her, either. The other woman had made it plain that she considered Joss to be very much her private property.

'I said nothing,' Joss corrected her. 'You were the one who made the claim. I simply . . .'

'Implied that it was correct,' Nell cut in brittly. 'Joss, whether she has or has not shared your bed isn't really relevant. When you first proposed to me, I was too confused to think it through properly.'

'You mean you were too relieved to have the burden of worrying about the tax bills lifted from your shoulders to think about having to endure my lovemaking,' he said harshly. 'Well, it's too late for maidenly shrinking now, Nell. Do you really think I'd let you make a fool of me by calling the whole thing off? Oh, no . . .'

'You can't stop me,' Nell told him bravely, and then quailed beneath the look he gave her.

'Oh, I think I can,' he said softly, and it was only when he reached her for that she realised exactly what it was he intended to do.

She cried out as she felt the bed depress beneath her, trying to squirm away from him, but the gold eyes held an implacable purpose that warned her that there would be no escape.

'If our first child arrives a little early, I shan't mind, and you won't take the risk of sullying the family name by giving birth to a bastard, will you, Nell?'

'No, please, Joss . . . don't do this. I will marry you. I . . .'

'Words, Nell, and you've already proved to me that they mean nothing. This way, there'll be no more second thoughts.' He imprisoned her with one arm, while he stripped her with his free hand. She refused to struggle or to give in to the frantic fear

thudding her heart. She had been weak and stupid
enough already. If he expected her to cry or plead, if
he expected anything from her other than unmoving
acceptance of his superior strength . . .

When she had imagined their first night together,
she had pictured herself dressed more romantically;
the scene set with flickering candles, her body
relaxed perhaps by champagne. Now the only feeling she could experience was one of sheer shock,
laced with humiliation as she saw herself revealed to
Joss's unreadable gaze in the clean but most definitely unglamorous underwear that had been chain-
store bought and was serviceable rather than attractive. She felt none of the arousal she had experienced
during the afternoon. None of the pleasure and
excitement, only a shocked resignation, laced with
misery.

She refused to close her eyes, but looked
steadfastly instead at a point beyond Joss's shoulder,
so that to feel the softness of the quilt which
unexpectedly covered her trembling body made her
look directly at him.

'There's really no need to be nervous. I'm not
doing this to hurt you, Nell, but I won't take the risk
of losing you now to Williams or anyone else.'

Of losing her . . . Of losing the title, didn't he
mean? But she held back the bitter words and
swallowed painfully, doing nothing to correct his
apparent belief that she was in love with David.

She was free now, and could have got up quite
easily, but she doubted if she did that she would get
as far as the door, and she wasn't going to heap
further humiliation on her own head by being
dragged back to the bed, which she was quite sure he
would do.

Joss was ruthless; she had always known that, and
at the back of her mind perhaps she had also feared
it.

She tried to blot out the alien sounds of a man un-
dressing, refusing to turn her head and look at him,
even when she heard him laugh softly.

'Modest, Nell? What an anachronism you are in
these times. Truly a pearl beyond price.'

Sure that he was mocking her, Nell turned her
head sharply, her eyes widening in shocked awareness of his maleness as he bent to flip back the cover
and join her on the bed.

His body was tanned, or at least almost all of it
was, she acknowledged, remembering that brief
strip of paler flesh that had drawn her gaze so
betrayingly. It was also packed with muscles that
moved and rippled beneath his skin, making him
suddenly seem totally different from the other men
she knew.

As he moved close to her she was immediately
aware of the scent of his skin, and the clean, fresh
smell of some masculine soap underlaid by a more
primitive, faint odour of maleness, musky and alien,
heightening her awareness of him, making him at
the same time more vulnerable, as human as she was
herself, and also more intimidating in the way that
such a powerfully sensual man must always be
slightly awe-inspiring.

He bent his head close to her own, so close that
she could see the pores of his skin and the shape of
the bones that underlay it.

'Don't be afraid,' he said as he had said before.
'I'm not doing this to hurt you, Nell, but you must
see that I can't lose you now.'

Oh, yes, she could see it, and for the space of a

heartbeat she contemplated telling him the truth, letting him see how impossible their marriage would be for her with the burden of her love for him, but she stopped herself, seeing the relentless determination darken his eyes, and wondering if he might not simply choose to use her love for him as another means of binding her to him.

What must it be like to want something so much that no human feelings, however intense, could stand in the way of that wanting?

Ambition . . . Once, long ago, her forebears must have possessed it . . . must have fought for it and killed for it; but none of that need burned her blood with its icy heat. She had been brought up to uphold the traditions of her name and family, but she knew that she would gladly abandon them all if in doing so she could gain Joss's love.

His mouth touched her skin, his fingers feather-light as they smoothed the hair back off her face.

'You're trembling. There's really no need, Nell.'

No need for him, maybe.

His hands traced the sharp jut of her collarbone, his mouth teasing its way across the smooth curve of her jaw.

'You've lost weight,' he murmured against her mouth.

She was surprised he'd noticed, but forebore to say so. Apart from the light caress of his hands and mouth, he wasn't touching her at all, and when she looked at him it seemed to Nell that just for a moment there was a grave tenderness in his eyes.

'This isn't how I intended it to be, Nell. But who knows . . . maybe it's for the best. At least this way the ordeal will soon be behind you. What did they tell you about this when you were growing up, Nell?

That it was a lady's duty to submit to her husband
and to provide him with sons?'

The wry tone of his voice hurt her. Did he really
think her so cut off from reality . . . so archaic? Did
he actually believe that at twenty-four she had
neither the intelligence nor the insight to form her
own views and beliefs?

'I might be physically inexperienced, Joss,' she
told him quietly, 'but that doesn't mean that I'm not
aware that sex can be one of life's richest pleasures.'

She chose the word deliberately, forcing herself to
look directly at him and not flinch beneath the look
in his eyes.

'If that's so, why have you never experienced it, I
wonder?' She hesitated for a moment and then said
coolly, 'I don't know. Maybe because as yet I
haven't met a man who's made me want to?'

'Is that a challenge, Nell? Because if so . . . ' She
tensed as she felt his fingers bite slightly into her
arms.

But before she could even draw a breath to protest
his mouth was on hers, caressing it into sensuous
recognition of his mastery as he teased and coaxed
from her an unwilling response.

She tried to fight back the tide of sensation beating
through her, but desire, once aroused, as she was
beginning to discover, was not so easily dammed.

Joss's mouth left hers, and she saw him studying
its soft shape before he traced it tantalisingly with his
forefinger. As though it had a mind of its own, her
flesh clung to his. She made a tiny sound deep in her
throat, unconcsciously trying to prolong the physical
contact, and, as though it was a sign he had been
waiting for, Joss moved, covering her body with his,
saying her name huskily and unevenly as he kissed

her again. This time not gently or carefully, his hand sliding from her arms to her body, shaping it beneath him as he sucked fiercely on her tongue, drawing it into his mouth, caressing it, until Nell was driven by her need to reciprocate the caress, not even realising what she had done until she felt the groan he stifled in his throat vibrate against her fingertips.

She stopped abruptly then, shocked by her own lack of self-protection. What had happened to her determination not to betray how she felt? She trembled tensely beneath the heat of his body, waiting for him to make some flippant, taunting comment, but instead he moved her so that he could slide his hand along her ribcage and cup her breast, his voice rough against the ear.

'I want you, Nell.'

And he moved so that she could feel the truth of his statement in the arousal of his body, not intimidating at all, she realised in surprise, but pleasurably awesome, making her feel intensely female and powerful that she should be able to have this effect on him.

Beneath his light caress her breasts ached, her nipples tight and hard. When he brushed one softly with his thumb, fierce darts of sensation pulsed through her, making her insides ache in unexpected recognition of her need.

'Joss.' She said his name uncertainly, an un-spoken plea darkening her eyes as she looked at him. She had been prepared to want him, but she hadn't realised it would be like this. She hadn't realised that just this brief physical contact would make her ache for him with an intensity that went beyond pride and self-respect; that just that brief taste of him would

make her want to adore his body with her hands and
mouth.

She found it extraordinary that she had never felt
like this before; never suspected herself of being
capable of this depth of physical abandonment;
never known how powerfully strong her own desires
could be.

'Shush,' he told her. 'It's all right.' And his voice
rasped slightly, raw and very different from the cool,
often remote tone she was used to.

'It's all right, Nell,' he repeated thickly. 'I just
want to look at you . . . to touch you.'

And he eased back the duvet so that the thin light
from the new moon filtered through the darkness
and bathed her skin in a fragile silver-white beam
that seemed to highlight all the shadows and curves
of her flesh, making them mysterious and alluring
and, even to her own eyes, unfamilar.

Had her waist always had that narrow, vulnerable
curve; her breasts that unexpectedly voluptuous fullness crowned with nipples whose aureoles were
surely darker and larger than she recalled?

Even the curve of her hip was offered up to the
moon's mysterious invoking light, the graceful line
of her thigh and the delicacy of her ankle-bone all
known to her, and yet in some way unknown, and,
against their silvery paleness, absorbing rather than
reflecting the light like her flesh, was the male darkness of Joss's body.

She sucked in a shallow breath as she gazed at the
indentation of his waist, the flat hardness of his
buttocks, the strength of his thigh where it covered
her own flesh; a statement of ownership and
possession.

She shivered suddenly, raising a rash of goosebumps from her throat to her hip.

Her breath locked in her chest as Joss stroked her skin with one finger, smoothing delicately over the sensitive flesh, from her collarbone down over her breast.

When he reached its flushed crest it seemed to Nell that he trembled—or was it her?—and then he said thickly, 'Oh, God, Nell!'

And for the first time in her life she experienced the tumultuous sensation aroused by a man's mouth against her breast, as Joss gently sucked her nipple into his mouth. She must have cried out, although she wasn't aware of it. Joss tensed and then released her, covering her moist nipple with his hand, as though he couldn't bear to relinquish all contact with her.

She was bathed in fine perspiration, her eyes dark and shocked.

'I never knew it would feel like that,' she said huskily, barely able to focus on him, conscious only of the intensity of what she was feeling.

He caressed the swollen tip of her breast and she shuddered violently, unable to control the response that convulsed her.

'It's all right,' Joss told her. 'It's just that some women have exceptionally sensitive breasts, so sensitive in fact that . . .' He broke off, and Nell wondered if he knew about the pulsing ache tormenting her lower body . . . if he knew exactly what effect he was having on her . . . A wave of shame washed over her. How could she be so uncontrolled, so, so . . .

As though he knew what she was thinking, Joss groaned and gathered her against him so that the sensitive crests of her breasts rubbed against his chest, making her moan softly.

'It's all right, Nell . . . it's all right . . .' he
reassured her, but Nell felt far from all right. Her
whole body ached and pulsed, and she almost cried
out with frustration when he slowly released her and
moved away from her.

He didn't want her, after all. He had changed his
mind about making love to her. Where she should
have felt relief, she felt only anguish.

She closed her eyes and then opened them
abruptly as she felt Joss cup her breasts in his hands,
shuddering wildly, as he caressed one and then the
other with his mouth, sucking gently at first and
then far less gently as he felt her abandoned
response.

Her spine arched, her nails digging into his
shoulders, leaving tiny crescent marks as she cried
out her pleasure.

She was barely aware of Joss lifting her, moving
her and even touching her, other than to dimly
recognise above the fierce crescendo of her need that
the gentle stroke of his fingers against the most
intimate part of her soothed and comforted the
tormenting ache aroused by the hot drag of his
mouth against her breasts.

It was only when he moved and lifted her on top of
him that she realised what he was doing, and tensed.

'It's all right, Nell,' he told her. 'This way, you'll
be the one in control. You'll be able to see as well as
feel everything that's happening.'

Never in her wildest imaginings had she dreamed
her initiation would be like this; that she would know
the heady power of delicately absorbing his flesh
within her own, and seeing in his face what she was
doing to him.

And then abruptly their roles changed and she cried out as she felt the sharp flash of pain, the sound silenced by Joss's mouth as he kissed her and soothed her, seeming to know exactly when it faded, his hand on her hips tutoring her body to the rhythm of his.

She felt within her an urgent reaching out, a desperate striving for some unknown goal, which despite her need remained elusive even though her body shook and trembled with her frantic attemtps to reach it.

'Gently, Nell, gently,' Joss said hoarsely against her ear, and miraculously he was right; as she allowed her body to respond to his tutoring, she felt the tiny ripples begin and then swell until they surged and exploded in mind-destroying eddies of pleasure that left her weak and drained.

She felt the pulsing release of Joss's body within her own, and wondered vaguely if she would conceive. It hardly seemed important in the light of her discovery of how pleasurable physical satisfaction could be.

But if she didn't love Joss, would she have felt like this? Somehow she doubted it. The thought was instantly sobering. She felt Joss move beside her, and turned the head to see that he was getting dressed. Of course. Now that his purpose was accomplished, there was little point in him staying, she reflected miserably. She was not what he was used to and no doubt she had bored him. She had often heard it said that experienced men did not particularly like making love to virgins.

Joss was half dressed now. She, too, ought . . . but, as she moved, Joss stopped her, pulling on his shirt, and leaving it unfastened as he leaned down and, wrapping the quilt round her, lifted her off the bed.

'Joss . . . What are you doing?'

'Taking you to your room,' he told her. 'Making love for the first time can be physically and emotionally exhausting.'

'That doesn't mean that I can't walk to my bed-room,' Nell told him.

'True.' He smiled at her, and she had an over-whelming urge to trace the curled line of his mouth, which she fought to resist. 'But, since I can't spend the night with you, allow me at least this indulgence, Nell.'

She looked at the bed, and bright colour flooded her skin as he said calmly, 'Don't worry. I'll see to everything before I go.'

He remembered which was her room, although Nell saw that his mouth tightened as he looked round it.

'Why *is* there no heating?'

'Aunt Honoria didn't approve of heating in the bedrooms,' she told him primly as he put her down on her bed.

She wondered if he would kiss her, and was dis-appointed when he didn't.

As he straightened up, he said softly, 'It's too late for second thoughts now, Nell.' His hand pressed lightly against her stomach, and it was almost as though her womb actually contracted beneath his touch.

She fell asleep still wrapped in the quilt, not waking until it was daylight, wondering frantically what on earth Mrs Booth would have thought if she had happened to walk into her bedroom.

Nell had never in her life slept in the nude . . . had never in her life had the kind of betraying small bruises on her skin that her body displayed now. Had never in her life experienced the enervating lassitude that possessed her limbs, nor known this faint soreness.

All the time she was dressing she thought about Joss. About how he had touched her . . . about how her had aroused her . . . about how he had made love to her.

And her heart sang. Perhaps their marriage might work out, after all . . . perhaps . . .

# CHAPTER EIGHT

WITHIN hours Nell had come crashing back down to
earth. When she saw the chauffeur-driven Rolls pull
up in front of the house her stomach muscles
tightened pleasurably in anticipation of Joss's
appearance, only it wasn't Joss who stepped out of
the immaculately polished car, it was Fiona.

Stifling her disappointment, Nell went downstairs
to meet her.

As always, the other woman was immaculately
and expensively dressed. Nell, who had been
helping Mrs Knowles to fit the newly made covers
on to the old furniture, was wearing one of her new
pairs of jeans and a sweatshirt.

Under Liz's approving eye, the outfit had seemed
both practical and attractive; now with Fiona
studying her with amused contempt, it merely
looked scruffy.

She had come, she explained, to get Nell's
signature to some forms that were required to open
the bank accounts Joss was organising for her.

As Nell led the way into the library, she thought
that Fiona looked as smug as a cream-fed cat, and
the other woman's self-assurance only added to her
own feelings of inadequacy.

Feelings which had doubled and tripled overnight
to such an extent that she was badly in need of Joss's
reassurance. As he had promised he would do, he
had left the bedroom pristine neat.

She signed the forms quickly, without speaking to

Fiona, but something must have given her away
because she said in evident amusement, 'Poor Joss.
He was rather apprehensive about coming to see you
today, after last night.'

Nell felt her heart thud and leap against her chest
wall.

She kept her head bent over the papers, but she
knew her hand shook as Fiona studied them and
pointed out where she had omitted one signature.

She knew, too, that the other woman had seen the
betraying tremor.

'Poor darling. He wasn't sure if he was going to
be able to go through with it. I told him, it's
normally the woman who has to lie back and think of
England. I told him to close his eyes and imagine
that . . .'

Nell couldn't take any more. She stood up
quickly, scattering papers all over the desk. She was
breathing quickly, and she knew her face had lost all
its colour.

Handing Fiona the signed papers, she said with
quiet dignity, 'I believe you've got everything you
came for. Please leave.'

And then she did something she did very, very
rarely. She touched the bell beside the desk, and
when Johnson appeared, looking rather surprised
and concerned, she asked him to show Fiona
out.

She saw from the other woman's face that she was
not pleased, and it gave her a brief stab of satisfaction, but that soon disappeared once she was
alone and forced to confront what Fiona had said to
her.

She could hardly believe that Joss had actually
discussed something so private and personal with his

secretary, no matter what their relationship, and
Joss had told her that they were not lovers. Had he
lied to her? Not about that . . . but perhaps, by
omission, about Fiona's feelings for him? He must
know she was in love with him and, knowing that,
he had voluntarily betrayed Nell to her. How could
he have humiliated her in such a way? Humiliated
them both?

Last night, she had thought she had seen, if not
love, then at least tenderness and concern in his
eyes; now she knew how cruelly self-deceptive she
had been.

And it wasn't entirely Joss's fault. He had told her
why he was making love to her, warned her that
there was only one reason; but she, self-deluded fool
that she was, had thought that the desire of his body
was for her as a person . . . as a woman.

Now she knew she was wrong. Oh, but how could
he have discussed her with Fiona like that? Have
allowed the other woman to know how little he
desired her, especially after they had agreed that
they would behave like any other couple in love?

She couldn't marry him now. She *wouldn't* marry
him now. And then she looked around the room and
remembered her promise to her grandfather. Her
hand touched her stomach lightly and she trembled.
Supposing she *had* already conceived Joss's child?
He was right, she was not strong enough to bring up
her child alone . . . outside the bonds of marriage.
She admired those women who could, for their
strength and their self-reliance, but her strengths
were not theirs. There was no escape for her.

Half-way through the morning a man arrived and
announced that he had been sent by Joss to install a
central heating system. Despite the fact that, in the

winter, Nell hated the cold dampness of the house and her great-aunt's belief that cold fresh air was necessary and healthy, she immediately felt resentful that Joss should have arranged something without consulting her.

She got Johnson to show the man round and went back to her self-imposed task of cleaning the silver.

Normally for wedding buffets she hired cutlery and china, but for her own . . . There were cast canteens of initialled family silver dating back to late Victorian times. The Georgian silver had been sold by her grandfather and never replaced, but even the Edwardian sets would probably be valuable now, she reflected as she and Mrs Booth worked companionably side by side cleaning it.

Somewhere in one of the cupboards was the dinner-service which had been specially commissioned for her great-grandmother's wedding. She suspected that it was probably packed away in the attic, and, as she remembered from her great-aunt's stories, there had been over one hundred and fifty guests at the wedding breakfast. The days were gone when people commissoned a dinner-service especially for one special event, even if once it had been common practice among the wealthy.

Nell had never seen the service. She knew it was Spode and suggested to the housekeeper that they try to find it. She had already had a telephone call from the dealer who was going to view the china, and he was calling round later in the afternoon on behalf of his client, so that too had to be washed and displayed, and Nell chose to place it on the table in the formal dining-room.

'Hideous, isn't it?' she commented when she and the housekeeper had finished this task. 'It's hard to believe it's so valuable. Lucky for me, though.'

Mrs Booth was as well aware as the rest of the staff of Nell's financial problems, and, knowing that she was not the kind to gossip, Nell added quietly, 'You see, with the money I'll get from this, I'll be able to pay for the wedding myself. And for the work I've organised on the house. Perhaps it's old-fashioned of me.'

If Mrs Booth found it odd that Nell should want to spend what little capital she had when she was on the point of marrying an extremely wealthy man, she kept it to herself. Nell couldn't really explain even to herself just why she felt she had to make this final gesture of indpendence. She only knew that she could not allow Joss to pay for her wedding dress, for the new clothes she had bought, and the new underwear that Liz had slyly insisted on adding to their purchases. Had she been pressed to give a reason, she would have had to say that it just wasn't the proper thing to do, but there was more to it than that. Perhaps even a desire to prove to Joss that though he might have bought the house and the title . . . he could not buy her.

It was just after three-thirty when the antiques dealer arrived. Nell took him straight through to the dining-room where the china was displayed, and then stood patiently to one side while he examined every piece.

'It's excellent,' he pronounced at length. 'My client will be delighted. I'm empowered to offer you . . .' and he named a sum that made Nell almost gasp in delighted shock. 'That is for the full set, of course. It's very rare to find one in such good condition. This one looks as though it has barely been used.'

Nell just stopped herself from telling him that the reason why it was in such good condition was that no one had liked it; it seemed hardly politic in view of the vast sum he was offering her for it.

She and Mrs Booth helped him pack it up carefully, the bankers' draft he had made out in Nell's own name carefully locked away in the desk drawer.

They were just wrapping the final few pieces, Nell on her knees at the dealer's side, in the dining-room, when Joss walked in.

The sight of him, so unexpected when she hadn't expected to see him and was unprepared for the jolting shock of pleasure seeing him always gave her, robbed her both of colour and breath, so that she could only kneel there staring up at him while he surveyed the chaos on the floor with frowning concentration.

'What's going on here? Doing a moonlight flit, Nell?' he demanded harshly.

Her colour flooded back, and the dealer discreetly got up, picking up the last box.

'Thank you again, and if there's anything else you wish to dispose of . . .'

He handed her his card, gave Joss a brief smile, shook hands formally with Nell and was gone, hurriedly escorted away by Mrs Booth.

'What exactly is it you're disposing of Nell, and why? I wonder. Do you suspect I'm going to make a mean husband? Or is there another reason . . a nest egg? A little something tucked away for the future? Running away money, Nell? Is that what this is all about?'

He was angry, bitterly, furiously angry, and he had no right to be.

'Hasn't it occurred to you that morally, if not
legally, the contents of this house are now at least
half mine. Is that why you're selling them now,
Nell? Before we're married? What else are you
arranging to dispose of? I wonder . . . perhaps I
ought to have done an inventory . . .'

The unfairness of his allegations silenced her.

'Do you really think I'm going to stand by and let
you sell off our son's heritage? If you wanted money,
Nell, you should have asked me.'

It was too much . . . much too much. Her nerves,
strained already beyond endurance, suddenly
snapped, and with them her frail hold on her
temper.

It blazed up inside her wildly, gloriously, bursting
past her self-control, ignoring the eagle glare of
Joss's eyes.

'How dare you dictate to me what I do with my
own possessions, Joss? And besides——' she added
scornfully, hating him for his autocratic disdain,
hating him for not loving her when she loved him,
hating him for his assumed right to dictate to her
what she did, and hating him most of all for
betraying her to Fiona. She wanted to hurt him . . .
she needed to hurt him, and in the intensity of that
momentary need, fuelled by temper and exhaustion,
she chose the most powerful weapon she had, and
said scornfully, 'Besides, anyone with the slightest
pretensions to knowledge could have told you that
that particular dinner-service is of no historic value
at all. In fact it's just a vulgar, overgilded Victorian
dinner service, of a type that no one other than a too
wealthy social climber would want to own. As *you*
would have known if . . .'

'If what?' he demanded dangerously, and too late

she realised just where her temper and pain had led her.

'If what, Nell?' he pressed, and the very quietness of his voice added to her alarm, but she couldn't back down now. Not entirely.

'If you knew anything at all about china,' she finished bravely, ignoring the fact that, until the dealer had told her, she herself had had no idea of the dinner-service's potential value.

Seeing his silence, feeling the rage emanating from him, she added huskily, 'Joss, it was hideous. If I'd been selling the Sèvres, or the Worcester, then I could understand your feelings . . .'

He hadn't moved, his body so tense it was almost rigid, his bones standing out sharply in the harshness of his face.

'Could you? But then a man like me could never be expected to know the difference, could he? Just as well you told me it was hideous, Nell, otherwise I might have embarrassed us both by admiring it. After all, it was old, and to people like me—common, ordinary people, without the benefit of your kind of background—anything old must be valuable, mustn't it?'

She hated the cynical scorn in his voice. Hated the way he was looking at her, as though she were beneath contempt, but he had hurt her bitterly by discussing her with Fiona, and there could be no excuses for that kind of betrayal, none at all.

'I suppose that's why you got rid of my interior designer, was it? You felt you couldn't trust her taste. After all, I'd chosen her. She might have recommended all those naff little touches so beloved by the *nouveaux riches*.'

He saw her wince and eyed her savagely.

'Is that why you refused to speak to me on the telephone this morning, Nell? I thought at the time it was just maidenly confusion . . . a little probably very natural embarrassment . . . but I was wrong, wasn't I? Your refusal was probably far more likely to have been made out of sheer self-disgust at the thought of having actually enjoyed making love with a man like me,' he added acidly.

'Joss! No!' she cried out. 'You're wrong. I . . .'

He stopped half-way across the room and looked at her. There was no mercy in the coldness of his eyes, no compassion or relenting.

'Am I? I don't think so. You were quite right, Nell. You and I don't know enough about one another, but it's too late to cancel things now. You could be and probably are carrying my child . . .'

'And if I'm not?' Nell asked him, through lips stiff with pain.

His face darkened, the golden eyes glittering dangerously.

'If you're not, then it will by my duty to remedy that omission just as quickly as I can. After all, that is the whole purpose of this marriage, isn't it, Nell? That between us we produce an heir for this house and my wealth?'

He said it bitterly, cuttingly, as thought *he* was the one with the grievance, as though it was she who was the betrayer and not him, and it was only long after he had gone, and she was sitting wearily in the coldness of the small sitting-room, reflecting on the savagery of his reaction to the sale of a mere dinner-service, that she remembered that that hadn't been the sole reason for his rage. He had mentioned a telephone call. A telephone call she was supposed to have refused, but which in fact she had never received. A lie on his part . . . or a deliberate omission on someone else's. His secretary's for instance.

Her whole body went cold. She looked at the telephone on the sofa table, and was actually reaching for it, before she acknowledged the pointlessness of such an exercise. What did it matter whether he had telephoned her or not? He had still discussed her with Fiona; had still revealed to the other woman that they had spent the night together . . . Had still allowed her to believe that he had found no pleasure in making love to her, even if he had not told her so directly.

This afternoon she had seen with disastrous clarity what their life together was going to be, and it had appalled her. Joss had seen it too, but he was refusing to let her go, and if there was a child . . .

Perhaps the wedding could be delayed until they could be sure . . . but, even as the thought formed, she knew that Joss would never agree. He was determined to marry her, and he wasn't going to allow anything to stop him now.

On her way to bed, she changed direction and, instead of going to her own room, went into the master suite instead.

Now it was almost finished: the carpet had been cleaned and relaid; the new bed-hangings were in place, the sitting-room furnished.

She walked up to the bed, touching it, finding it almost impossibe to believe that it was here, on this bed last night that Joss had made love to her . . . had made her believe that he might actually come to care for her . . . that he did desire her . . .

And yet now she could barely believe that any of it had happened. It was as though it had happened to someone else, and not to herself . . . All the pleasure and happiness she had experienced in his arms was gone.

She felt empty and alone . . . drained of the ability to do anything other than merely exist.

# CHAPTER NINE

'IT STILL isn't too late to change your mind, Nell.'

The quietly serious voice of her friend made Nell turn away from her contemplation of the gardens to smile wryly at her.

'It's always been too late,' she told her. In less than three hours she and Joss would be standing in front of the vicar, sharing the solemnity of the marriage service, making promises and vows that they both knew could not be kept.

'Nell, you look dreadful. You're so thin and pale, and Joss doesn't look much better. What's happened between you?'

Liz and Robert had arrived the previous day. Joss had joined them for dinner in the evening and Nell knew that the strain between Joss and herself must have been immediately and painfully obvious to her friends.

Since the night they had made love they had barely spoken. When he came to the house, she offered him the coolness of her cheek to kiss and not her mouth; when he touched her, however lightly, she instinctively withdrew behind a brittle shell of politeness. Where another woman might have wept and stormed and finally demanded to know how he dared to discuss their most intimate moments together with someone else, Nell took refuge in hauteur and silence. It was the ony way she knew of defending herself, and, and after the first couple of occasions when she had coolly rebuffed him, Joss

had become as remote towards her as she was to
him.

And last night . . . not even for the sake of
maintaining some sort of pretence in front of her
oldest friend had she been able to stop herself from
shivering when Joss had greeted her with a kiss that
had punished her mouth for its rejection of him,
while his hand against her throat and jaw stopped
her from turning away.

This morning, her wedding morning, she had
been up and dressed long before the rest of the
household, inspecting the ballroom where she and
the rest of the staff had spent the best of the last two
days preparing for the reception.

The sprung floor gleamed; thin, sharp autumn
sunlight shone through the windows; the tables and
chairs hired for the occasion were all in place; the
team of florists had worked long into the late afternoon decorating the room with swags of fresh flowers
and silk ribbons, garlanding the top table with them
and putting soft posies of them on each table.

The church had been decorated in the same style:
pretty, softly pastel flowers in seemingly casually
arranged bunches that had taken skilled hands many
hours to fashion.

Nell was determined that, above everything else,
Joss would have no cause to complain that her
organisation of their wedding was less efficient than
his secretary's.

And besides, working hard had kept her mind an
all too necessary heartbeat away from snapping
under the burden of the knowledge she carried.

Was Joss already steeling himself for tonight?
Knowing that he must make love to her and also
knowing that the only way he could do so would be

by pretending she was someone else?

The thought made her want to be violently ill.

'Nell . . . it's time to go and get ready,' Liz warned her, touching her arm lightly.

Her dress was hanging in her room, her suitcase was packed beside the bed for the honeymoon destination Liz had told her excitedly that Joss wanted to keep a secret. Liz had packed her clothes, not allowing her to see what she had chosen. No doubt the venue would be some expensive holiday resort where they would be safely surrounded by other people so that Joss would not have to endure her company any more than was strictly necessary.

Liz had driven her into town straight after breakfast—a meal that Nell hadn't been able to touch, despite everyone's complaints that she was getting too thin—to have her hair done, and now it floated around her shoulders in a soft, pale cloud.

There were to be no bridesmaids, a fact which had made Joss frown until Nell pointed out to him that, with her own stepsister refusing the role, she could hardly choose someone else.

Liz helped her dress. Nell knew that downstairs the staff and everyone who had helped in the preparations for the wedding were waiting excitedly to see her, she also knew that she owed it to them to go downstairs so that they could, but an odd inertia had enveloped her and, as she stood docilely in front of the mirror while Liz fiddled with her head-dress, she felt as though her life had suddenly come to a full stop and that she would be more than happy if she never moved a foot outside this room.

Like some sort of latter-day Miss Havisham, she reflected wryly, remembering her Dickens . . . only she of course had never married. She had been

deserted before the wedding. What if Joss chose to
desert her? What if . . .?

'Nell, it's time to leave.'

She focused on Liz with difficulty, seeing the
concern and worry in her friend's eyes.

'The car's here.'

She was travelling to the church in Joss's Rolls.
Her godmother's husband, the Lord Lieutenant of
the county, was giving her away.

Liz had tentatively offered Robert to perform this
service for her, and although Nell would have
preferred him she had gently refused. When Joss
had asked her why, she had told him coolly that she
had thought he would prefer her to be given away by
the Lord Lieutenant.

He had given her an odd look, she remembered,
something that was not quite a frown, but rather a
mingling of derision and pain.

But why? He was the one who had wanted this
lavish show . . . this large wedding. She would have
much preferred a quieter ceremony.

'Ashamed of me, Nell?' he had asked curtly,
when she had suggested it, and so she had calmly
followed his wishes.

'Nell.' She turned her head at the sound of her
friend's voice.

Liz was unclasping something from her neck; a
fine, thin gold chain that glinted in the light. A tiny
gold heart-shaped locket hung from it, decorated
with minute pearls.

'Something borrowed . . . something old . . .' she
said as she fastened it round Nell's throat.

Nell touched the locket and smiled wanly.

'Thanks.'

'Don't thank me. Joss gave it to me and told me to

make sure you wore it. He said it belonged to his great-grandmother.'

Absurdly, tears sprang into her eyes. She would never have imagined Joss to be capable of such an act of sentimentality. She touched the gold again, feeling it warm the coldness of her skin. And she was cold . . . icily so.

'You look beautiful,' she heard Liz whisper, and she sensed from her voice that her friend wasn't far from tears herself.

'We'd better go down.'

The staff, and the wives and children of the estate workers, were gathered in the hall, and for the first time since getting up Nell felt reality break through the distancing calm she had wrapped herself in as she heard the soft cries of pleasure and admiration from the women.

Her godmother stood at the back of the hall, smiling warmly at her. 'Nell, darling, you look wonderful. Such a lovely dress.'

At her side the Lord Lieutenant blustered, 'Yes, indeed. Be proud to give you away, Nell . . .'

He was a man of few words, but very kind-hearted, and Nell had known him since she was a child, but even so, that didn't alter the fact that neither she nor Joss had one single close relative attending the wedding.

There was a large crowd outside the church, the sun mellowing its ancient stone façade. The bells were pealing a clarion call of joy as Nell walked through the ancient lych gate on the Lord Lieutenant's arms.

Inside the church, it took her several seconds to adjust to the darkness after the bright sunshine outside.

The church was full, the groomsmen, all friends of Joss's, immaculately formal in their morning-dress.

The organist saw her . . . heads turned in an indistinguishable blur to Nell as she walked slowly towards the altar and Joss.

He didn't look round. His head was bent slightly, almost as though he were deep in prayer. The vicar smiled at her and reached out his hand to draw her forward. His flesh felt warm and dry, and she saw him give her a quick look of concern as he touched her icy fingers.

The ceremony began. Quiet words . . . solemn words; hymns conveying joy . . . prayers for the future. Promises and vows exchanged . . . the gold of Joss's ring on her finger, a heavy weight, chaining her, the cool touch of his mouth against hers; his eyes hard and wintry . . . bleak and without that fierce golden glow with which she was so familiar.

The vestry where she signed her maiden name for the last time. Neither she nor Joss had wanted any photographs taken in the church, and she was glad when she saw how much her hand trembled.

Her grandmother, Liz and Robert witnessed their signatures along with the Lord Lieutenant, and then back into the main body of the church; organ music swelling triumphantly to a fierce clamour, the cool dimness of the church . . . Joss's hand beneath her arm; the brilliance of the sunshine outside; the noise of the bells . . . people surrounding her, laughing, congratulating her . . . admiring her dress . . . strangers . . . none of whom could touch that cold, bitter place deep in her heart where she knew she had just desecrated the most moving ceremony there could be. For the rest of her life, she would be surrounded by these strangers and others like them, people alien to her as she was to them . . . people with eyes like cruel, sharp knives that stabbed into her, and then Joss was clearing a way to the waiting Rolls, and she was cocooned inside its warmth, her dress carefully tucked in with her by his chauffeur.

Joss himself sitting next to her, not looking at her, even when he said quietly, 'You wore it, then.'

For a moment she thought he was talking about her dress, and then she realised he meant the locket.

'Yes . . .'

And those were the only words they spoke, not just during the short drive back to the house, but throughout the wedding breakfast that followed.

The meal was everything that Nell had intended it should be, but that knowledge gave her no pleasure, not even when she saw the looks of surprise and in some cases chagrin in the eyes of Joss's colleagues and their wives.

At the far end of the room wedding presents had been stacked on an empty table. Soon the speeches and toasts would be over and then would come the nightmare of circulating among their guests.

The best man, to whom Nell had only been introduced earlier in the week, as he had been abroad on business, gave a witty speech; at least Nell assumed it must have been, because everyone else laughed, but she didn't hear a word. She felt as though all her senses were frozen; as though she was somehow cut off from everyone else, and living in a world completely her own.

The best man was reading telegrams, and Nell stiffened suddenly as she heard him saying, ' "To Joss and Eleanor with our love and best wishes for their future. From all the family''—and it's signed with far too many names for me to read out.'

Joss waited until the speeches were over to ask her curtly, 'How did my family know about this?'

'I wrote to them,' Nell responded defiantly. 'They *are* your family, Joss. As you said, they didn't want to come to the wedding, but I'm hoping that they will come and visit us later.'

'Visit us . . here? God, have you any idea how out of place they'll feel?'

'Only if we make them,' Nell told him, persisting stubbornly. 'Joss I wanted to get in touch with your mother, but . . .'

'Forget it,' he told her harshly. 'She's built herself a new life in Canada with a new family, and she doesn't want to be reminded of the past, and especially my role in it.'

He saw her face.

'Save your pity for someone who genuinely needs it,' he told her drily. 'She might be my mother, Nell, but only anatomically. There's no emotional bond between us. She was sixteen when she gave birth to me, for God's sake . . . only a child herself. There's no point of contact between us, and both of us prefer it that way. My *grandmother* was my mother, and I mourned her far more than I did the girl who gave me birth.'

'But, Joss . . .'

'I said forget it. Have the rest of my family here if you must . . . if you can, but leave it at that, Nell.'

She fell silent, wondering if he was telling her the truth or if he secretly did feel hurt by his mother's indifference towards him. Probably not, she acknowledged, remembering a woman she had known who had spent several years of her life looking for her own mother, only to discover when

she did that she had far, far more in common with
the adopted parents who had brought her up, and
who had confided in Nell that she sincerely wished
she had left the past alone.

They circulated among the guests, together and
then separately. David Williams approached Nell
uncertainly. He had a glass of champagne in his
hand, and she realised as he came up to her that he
was slightly tipsy.

'So, he's got you then, Nell,' he said, slurring his
words slightly. 'All nice and legally bought and paid
for . . .'

'David . . . please . . .'

She reached out to touch his arm, but suddenly
Joss was there between them, glowering at her.

'I was just congratulating Nell on her good
fortune,' David told him, trying to focus on him.

'You could have done that without touching her,'
Joss replied, and Nell was astounded by the muted
savagery in his voice.

As he led her away he told her curtly, 'Forget him,
Nell. You're married to me, and whatever he might
have meant to you before . . .'

'He meant nothing to me,' Nell protested, too
shocked to lie. 'He was just a friend, Joss . . .'

He looked at her, and as though something in her
face told him she was telling the truth he said drily,
'To you—but I doubt that he would have put his
feelings for you under the heading of friendship.
Don't encourage him, Nell.'

'I wasn't,' she told him crossly, glad of the
opportunity to escape from him when a business
colleague claimed his attention.

David seemed to have gone, and although there
were several people she ought to have sought out, to

talk to and thank, instead Nell sought refuge in the protective shadow of one of the deep windows.

Three women walked past her, their clothes spelling Knightsbridge and designer boutiques, elegant, enamelled women of a type she found particularly intimidating.

'Clever Joss,' she heard one of them purr. 'It took Alan hundreds of thousands of pounds and fifteen years to get a peerage in the Honours List; and of course it isn't hereditary. Joss has managed it in less than a tenth of that time and probably only had to spend half as much.'

So much for convincing the rest of the world that they had married for love, Nell thought, watching them walk right past her without even realising she was there.

'Nell.' She looked round to see Liz standing beside her, looking anxious. 'It's time you were getting changed.'

She allowed Liz to lead her upstairs like a docile doll, obediently putting on the light wool dress she had put out for her. Not one she recognised as having bought; it was bright red, with a matching, slightly shorter coat with a tiny black velvet collar.

'It's Valentino,' Liz told her. 'Joss chose it for you himself. He rang me a couple of weeks ago and asked me what size you are.'

Nell stiffened, aching to tear the dress off and throw it on the floor. She didn't want to wear clothes bought for her by Joss. God, wasn't it enough that he had bought her *home* . . . her family name . . . *herself* . . . did he have to make it clear to the world just what she was by buying her clothes as well?

'Nell, is something wrong? Don't you like it?'

She forced a smile.

'It's lovely,' she said unemotionally, and it was . . . quite the most beautiful outfit she had ever seen, and it fitted her perfectly, the red wool stunningly vibrant with her hair and skin.

Her hair no longer floated round her shoulders but had been brushed and confined in a pearl-studded snood and, as Liz offered her a lipstick that was almost exactly the same colour as her outfit, she reflected bitterly that Joss had left nothing to chance.

'Be happy, Nell,' Liz whispered tearfully as she bent to kiss her. 'And don't forget, I want to be godmama to your first . . .'

Nell gave her a wan smile, pausing at the door of her bedroom to look round it.

When she and Joss returned from wherever it was he was taking her, this would no longer be her room. This place that had been her refuge in times of despair while she was growing up . . . She swallowed hard on the uncomfortable lump in her throat and proceeded through the door.

Joss was waiting for her at the bottom of the stairs. He, too, had changed, into a fine silky wool suit with a discreet self-stripe and a cotton shirt which she suspected must have been made for him. Unlike the majority of the male guests she had invited, he had no old school tie to discreetly sport against his shirt, but the tie he was wearing was silk and striped, and the formality of his clothes made her even more aware of the abyss between them.

They said their goodbyes together, Nell only faltering once, when Joss's secretary came up to them, and kissed Joss full on the mouth.

Her lipstick had smeared his skin and she produced a pretty lace handkerchief and made a flamboyant show of wiping it off.

Joss was frowning, and Nell had the distinct impression that he wasn't pleased, but if Fiona was aware of his displeasure she gave no sign of it, smiling triumphantly at Nell and then ignoring her to link her arm through Joss's and press up against his side while she said softly, 'I've got your address . . . so if anything should need your attention . . .'

Nell saw several of the guests giving them speculative looks, and her skin burned hot and then cold with resentment.

When they were out of earshot of everyone else she said coldly to Joss, 'Was that really necessary?'

'What?' he asked her blandly.

'That . . . . that display with your secretary.'

She deliberately made her voice sound cold with distaste, refusing to allow her hurt to show through.

'Jealous, Nell, because she knows how to act like a woman and you don't?'

After that she couldn't do more than force herself to give a rather shaky smile at the last dozen or so of their guests who had come to wave them off.

They were travelling in the Rolls, but without the chauffeur. Joss might have made his way up the ladder from the bottom; he might not have had the advantages of birth, money and position that many of her acquaintances shared, but some things were either instinctive or simply not there, and could not be learned or assumed: like the easy way with which Joss dismissed his chauffeur and thanked the staff for their hard work; like the way he behaved to people around him, treating them with courtesy and consideration, whatever their position in life.

She had noticed that about him almost from the first time they had met; to her it was worth more than any amount of money, or centuries of family history.

So why, when it came to her, was he so icily polite . . . so . . . so hard? He must realise how diffcult all this was for her. In fact, she knew he did. Was this abrupt change in his manner because he now realised how very difficult their life together was going to be . . . because making love to her had opened his eyes to what a marriage without desire and certainly without love would mean?

She had been tempted to get into the back seat of the Rolls, but Joss opened the front passenger door for her. She looked up at him and saw the hardness of his mouth. His eyes seemed to be warning her that they had a fiction to maintain, although she was miserably sure that very few people had been deceived.

'I should try and sleep if I were you. We've got a long drive ahead of us,' he told her briefly as they pulled away from the house.

In other words, he didn't want to talk with her . . . He wanted to be left alone.

Nell couldn't sleep. She was far too tense, but at the same time she was conscious of being achingly exhausted. The interior of the Rolls was warm, and she wanted to remove her coat, but she felt she simply did not have the energy.

Where were they going? she wondered restlessly, her lacklustre gaze resting sombrely on the grey uniformity of the motorway. Heathrow most probably, and then a flight to some undoubtedly exotic and fashionable location, where they could simply pretend to be just another bored married couple. She leaned back in her seat and closed her eyes, obedient to Joss's suggestion.

A jumble of images danced behind her closed
eyelids. Her own reflection in the mirror in her
wedding dress . . . the noise of the reception . . . the
unfamiliar faces . . . the bright, artificial chatter of
the conversation of the men, deep-voiced discussions
on financial matters and deals, broken up by
disjointed phrases from the marriage service until it
ran through her mind like a jumbled and meaning-
less refrain.

What had she done? Oh God . . . what had she
done? Her eyes burned. Her body ached. She felt
slightly light-headed. She yawned once and then
again, her eyelids heavy, the almost noiseless purr of
the engine distinctly soporific.

'Nell.'

The hand on her shoulder was familiar and yet
alien, drawing her into a world she would rather not
inhabit, and so she resisted it, tensing against it as
the voice insisted she wake up.

Outside it was dark, the scene unfamiliar. They
were in the car, and to one side of them lay the bulk
of a large boat.

'Where are we? This isn't Heathrow . . .' she
said, confused.

'No. It's Dover. We're just about to board the
cross-Channel ferry.'

'Where are we going?'

She was still confused, still half asleep and unable
to assimilate what she was being told.

'Northern France,' Joss told her, his voice
clipped. 'The Château des Fleurs.'

He saw that the words meant nothing to her, and
as he set the car in motion to board the ferry he
explained that he was taking her to a château he

had rented in northern France, where they would
spend their honeymoon.

'A château? I thought we'd be going somewhere
like the Caribbean.'

'Is that what you'd have preferred, Nell?'

They were on board now, and she allowed him to
help her out of the car.

She dozed for most of the crossing and the drive
that followed it, waking up properly only when the
car stopped. It was dark outside. She could see a
pathway of silver cast by the moon, and the shapes
of formally clipped yews bordering a gravel path.

She felt stiff and uncomfortable, her head aching
slightly. At her side Joss said curtly, 'Just in case
you're interested, this château was once the home of
one of your ancestresses, Catherine de Chambertin.
It's still owned by a branch of the Chambertin
family, although it isn't their main home. It's one of
several châteaux which one can rent complete with
staff. Since not to have had a honeymoon would
have caused unnecessary comment, I thought you
would prefer this to a more commercialised venue.'

He had gauged her tastes exactly, and in different
circumstances—if she had never heard those spiteful
words of Fiona's for instance—she would have been
thrilled at the thought that he had taken so much
trouble in choosing this château.

As it was, all she could feel was an aching relief
that here at least she would be under no pressure to
play the role of the deliriously happy bride.

She got out of the car, refusing Joss's aid, watching the way his mouth tightened in anger at her
rebuff with a tiny spurt of rebellious satisfaction. Let
him see what it felt like to be rejected, if only in a
very small way.

The château was behind them, small and turreted, its sharp roofs glinting under the moonlight; a fairy-tale place of silver roofs and golden walls set against a backdrop of gardens whose splendour she could only imagine in the darkness.

The door opened and a man came out.

*'Monsieur.'* He gave Joss a brief, formal bow and then introduced himself. 'I am Henri. My wife, Gabrielle, and I will take care of you while you are with us.'

As he spoke, he removed their two suitcases, so ill-matched that Nell suspected he must either guess that they were newly married or suspect that they were lovers escaping for an illicit holiday together.

'If you will come this way . . .'

The hall was oval, with a marble-tiled floor and a curling flight of white marble stairs. The silk on the walls was fading in places, but was still very beautiful, the wrought-iron banister rail rich in fleur de lys and other emblems of heraldry, and as she studied it Nell remembered vaguely that there had been a suggestion that one of Catherine's relations had borne a child by a prince of the ruling family of France.

As they climbed the stairs, Gabrielle came to meet them. She was dark and very French, her glance snapping sharply over Nell's outfit, approving and admiring it. Her English was not quite as good as her husband's.

They had given them the state apartments, she told Nell. A light supper had been prepared for them as arranged by *monsieur,* and if there was anything else they required then they only had to ring.

*Petit déjeuner* would be served in the morning when they requested it, she added diplomatically, with a faint smile that made Nell's face burn.

The state apartments consisted of a sitting-room, a dining-room, a huge bedroom with two dressing-rooms and a bathroom, all of which were decorated in rich reds and gold, the Aubusson carpet in the sitting-room woven with the arms of the family.

Nell suspected that visitors were not normally given such opulent surroundings, and she wondered a little cynically how much Joss had had to pay to secure this special concession.

*Why* had he done it? To show her that there was nothing his money could not buy? Not even her family's past.

A cold buffet had been laid out in the dining-room, but the sight and smell of it made Nell feel acutely sick.

'It's been a long day, Joss,' she said huskily. 'If you don't mind, I think I'll go straight to bed.'

*If* he didn't mind? Of course he wouldn't mind. He'd probably be only too delighted, or so she thought, but she was wrong.

'If you're trying to tell me in a delicate and lady-like fashion that you want to sleep alone tonight, Nell, then I'm afraid you're going to be disappointed. In the first place, these rooms possess only one bed. In the second, despite the due pomp and ceremony with which we were married this morning, until our marriage is consummated, it cannot legally exist.' He saw her wince and his face hardened. 'Unfortunate, I agree, but a necessity, none the less. I shall endeavour to be as brief as possible,' he added with fine irony, and Nell thought bitterly of the many women who must have begged him to prolong every second they spent in his arms.

'I'll go and get undressed, then,' she said quietly, as polite and distant as a child.

He turned his head and she saw the gleam of mockery in his eyes.

'Surely that is the bridgroom's prerogative, Nell . . . to undress his bride.'

'Perhaps,' she agreed bravely, 'in a different kind of marriage. As you have already said, where we're concerned there seems little point in prolonging things . . .'

She saw that she had made him angry, although she had no idea why. Just for a second she thought he was actually going to reach out and take hold of her, but he pushed his hands into his pockets and turned away from her instead.

Her suitcase was on a small cupboard several feet away from the bed.

Joss had primed Liz well, she recognised as she saw the clothes her friend had packed. Her new separates, a couple of semi-formal dresses, low-heeled shoes, suitable for the country but still smart, a warm jacket and then, beneath her top clothes, several layers of underwear, but not underwear that Nell had ever bought.

She flushed slightly, her eyes widening as she removed the wispy satin and lace garments.

There was a nightdress in dusky rose satin, cut on the bias, and cut very low at the back, the bodice tiny cobwebs of the most exquisite lace through which her skin must surely be almost completely visible.

There was another . . . different in style but every bit as revealing.

She picked up the rose satin one with hands that trembled and went into the bathroom.

The bath was enormous, easily large enough for two people. Her body went hot at the thought and she refused to give in to the temptation to soak in the luxury of gallons of perfume-scented hot water, and showered briskly instead, rubbing her skin almost roughly with a towel until it glowed and stung slightly.

Her hair, released from its chignon, fell straight and shining; the nightdress slid easily over her head and clung to her skin.

On her, it was even more revealing than she had anticipated, dipping almost to the base of her spine at the back, the lace bodice cut to mould her breasts, the pearly sheen of her skin clearly discernible beneath the lace panels, the lace flowers that comprised the bodice designed in such a way so that two of the tiny pieces of lace that were the central stamens of the flowers were centred over her nipples, the panels so small that they didn't quite manage to cover the entire aureole of flesh. A deliberate oversight, Nell felt sure. Had Liz been aware of that when she chose it?

She heard Joss moving about in the bedroom, and wondered wildly if she dared dress in her clothes, but no . . . he would be expecting her to be undressed, to be . . .

Taking a deep breath, and suppressing the panic inside her, she opened the bathroom door.

Joss was standing with his back to her, facing the window. He had a glass in one hand and a bottle of champagne in the other.

Although she hadn't said a word, he must have heard her, because he turned round and said harshly, 'It's normally the bride who needs the fortifying glass of champagne, not the groom.'

He studied her body in its provocative veiling of satin and lace.

'Liz chose it,' Nell told him huskily, not wanting to think that she was stupid enough to believe that she could make him want her by wearing something so provocative.

'Wrong,' he told her succinctly. 'I chose it. I thought about how your skin would look against it, Nell,' he told her, ignoring her shock. 'Of how it would gleam like mother of pearl, iridescent as silk, warm and sweet as honey. But there's no warmth inside you, is there, Nell? At least not for me. Tell me something, my wife,' he demanded with sudden savagery. 'Does it really give you pleasure to look at me with such cool contempt? Is that your revenge for our marriage, Nell? Or perhaps this is how all well-bred wives behave. Like hell,' he ground out fiercely. 'Oh, you can look at me with your cool, disdainful eyes, but let me tell you something about your peers, my lady . . . Once between the sheets they're as hot and willing as . . .'

Nell couldn't stand any more. She cried out sharply, 'Stop it! Stop it, Joss. You were the one who wanted this marriage.'

'And you were the one who needed it,' he reminded her brutally, pouring himself a glass of champagne and drinking it quickly.

He held out the bottle to her, but she shook her head.

'No? Want to get the ordeal over with as quickly as possible, do you? Well, you'd better pray that if you aren't carrying my child already, by the end of tonight you are.'

He poured another glass of champagne and drank half of it, and then with a grimace he put the glass down.

'I've only ever had to do this once before—drink before I could make love to a woman. And she was my first. Take off your nightdress, Nell.'

He saw her shock and laughed unkindly. 'I thought you wanted to get this over as quickly as possible. If you keep that on that's not going to be possible. When I bought it for you it was with the intention of tasting every millimetre of flesh it exposed before I took it off you. Pathetic what traps our imaginations lay for us, isn't it . . .?'

He was, if not drunk, then at least tipsy, Nell recognised with shock, but then, like her, he had eaten nothing all day, and he was normally a very abstemious man. It made her skin crawl with self-disgust to realise that he had to get drunk before he could touch her. She had read about such things, but never anticipated she herself would experience them.

But Joss seemed unaware of her self-contempt. He was still looking at her, his eyes glittering hotly as he slowly studied her body.

He reached out and traced the delicate silk of one shoulder-strap with his thumb and, although he had not touched her there at all, Nell was uncomfortably conscious of the aroused tension in her breasts, her nipples pushing against the tiny shells of lace.

Even her breathing betrayed her agitation, she recognised frantically as she fought to control her response to him, trying to step back, but finding that doing so only brought him closer as he closed the gap between them.

'I knew you would look like this. Feel like this,' he said thickly, and, as though he knew exactly what she was feeling, he slowly traced the outer petals of the flower that covered her breast teasingly, narrowing the tormenting circles until the pad of his thumb touched the tiny ring of almost bare flesh that swelled against the lace stamens.

She wasn't cold, but she was shivering, Nell recognised, and so was Joss. That shocked her and she looked up at him. His eyes burned hot gold.

'Nell,' he muttered thickly, and she cried out as she felt his mouth close over her tormented flesh. Her whole body seemed to contract, her eyes unwittingly registering her shock and confusion that he could so easily arouse her. She forgot all the promises she had made to herself and clung desperately to him, making incoherent sounds of need and pleasure.

A long time later—or was it only minutes?—they lay together on the vast bed in a tangle of pleasure-sated limbs, the last tiny reverberations of sensation still pulsing through her body . . .

In the morning it was different. In the morning she remembered all that she should have remembered before letting Joss make love to her, and she was deliberately cool and distant with him, lashing herself with painful reminders of how much champagne he had had to drink before he could make love to her, and how the fierceness of his possession was a tribute to whoever he had been thinking about when he did make love to her, and not her herself.

The day was overcast, and dragged, both of them treating one another with the cool politeness of two strangers forced to endure one another's company.

After lunch Joss announced that he had some

work to do and Nell, taking the hint, announced that she would explore the gardens.

It was too cold to stay out for very long, and when she got back Joss was on the phone, frowning as he asked several brief questions.

When he replaced the receiver he was still frowning, but Nell didn't ask him if anything was wrong and when, later in the day after several more telephone calls, he announced that he was going to have to cut their honeymoon short and fly to New York, she made no demur.

# CHAPTER TEN

'YOU'RE not pregnant, then?'

Nell looked at her stepsister and fought against betraying the painful kick of pain twisting her stomach.

She and Joss had been married for eight weeks, and, as Grania had so rightly announced, she was not carrying his child. But then, it was hardly likely that she would be, not when he had not made love to her since their return from France.

In fact, he was hardly ever at home, spending long days in London, interspersed with increasingly frequent trips to New York. He looked tired and tense, and Nell suspected that he was bitterly regretting their marriage.

'Not yet,' she responded with false calm.

'Where is Joss, anyway? I thought he'd be here.'

'He's in New York.'

'Again? Perhaps he's got someone else there,' Grania suggested spitefully, adding when she saw Nell's colour change, 'Oh, come on, Nell, surely you don't expect him to be faithful to you?' She yawned. 'Well, I wish I'd known that before I came down here. I was hoping to coax him into giving me a sub. I've seen this darling fur coat—sable . . . and it is almost Christmas. I wonder if Joss will spend Christmas here or in New York,' she added maliciously.

'I really have no idea,' Nell retorted, her patience snapping.

She felt both relieved and guilty when Grania had gone, but her patience had been worn thin by the pressures within her marriage, and sometimes she didn't know which was worse, having Joss at home, or having him away. When he was at home he was distant with her, and, although they shared the same bedroom, since their honeymoon he had made no attempt to touch her. When he was away she ached for him to come home, hoping each time that somehow a miracle would occur and that he would come back wanting her, but of course it never did.

She was in the sitting-room making a list of Christmas cards when she heard the car. Thinking it might be Joss, she rushed to open the door, but it was Fiona who stood there, her appearance for once less than immaculate.

She came in, bringing with her the coldness of the November night.

'I know Joss isn't here . . . I just want to leave this for him. My resignation,' she added with a wintry smile. She saw Nell's surprise and laughed harshly. 'You *do* know that he's going to be declared bankrupt, don't you?' And then she said softly, 'So, he hasn't told you. I did wonder. Of course, he's been hoping to stave off complete disaster, but he's made several serious losses recently on the futures market. The banks are calling in all his loans, and he won't have the collateral to cover them.

'Poor Joss . . . now he'll just be another ex-millionaire . . .'

And as she said it Nell knew that the thought pleased her. She felt sick, and impotent, wanting desperately to refute what she was saying and yet knowing that she couldn't. Why hadn't Joss said something to her . . . shared his problems with her. . .?

'I must go—I've got a flight out to San Francisco at eleven. I've been offered a job there. Oh, by the way, Joss's solicitor says that there shouldn't be any problem getting the divorce through . . . not in the circumstances . . .'

With a final malicious smile she was gone, leaving Nell standing sickly against the door.

What divorce? Her own, of course. Joss was divorcing her . . . Well, she had been expecting it, but she had expected him to discuss it with her first . . . to tell her himself that it had been a mistake and not just simply let her find out from his secretary . . . his ex-secretary. And then she remembered what else Fiona had said to her. Joss was going to be declared bankrupt. She knew all too well what that would mean to him. It would destroy him. There must be a way it could be stopped. She knew less than nothing about Joss's financial affairs. All right, so he may have made several wrong decisions, but surely if he could just weather this crisis, he could recover . . . His bank would surely stand by him—and then Nell remembered Fiona saying that his banks were calling in his loans, because he didn't have enough collateral. Nell knew all too well what that meant, and then she remembered something else.

This house . . . this house could be used as security. She must find Joss and tell him . . .or better still tell the bank. It was almost ten o'clock at night . . . hours before she could contact the bank, she acknowledged fretfully. If only she knew where Joss was. If only he would get in touch with her, but he never contacted her when he was away and she had been too proud to ask him for an address or a telephone number.

Fiona might have known, but she was somewhere on her way to Heathrow.

Nell couldn't sleep. She was awake at dawn, and long before nine o'clock she was parked outside Joss's bankers' offices in Chester.

The girl on the enquiries counter didn't turn a hair when she asked to speak to the manager, even when Nell told her she didn't have an appointment.

'It is very urgent that I see him, though,' she stressed, praying that she would be able to do so.

Her prayers were answered. The manager came out of his office and smiled warmly at her. Far more warmly, surely, then a bank manager would smile at the wife of a potential bankrupt?

The moment she was in his office, Nell told him breathlessly why she had come.

He heard her out in silence, and then said noncommittally, 'I see.'

'Is it . . . is the house worth enough to . . . to cover my husband's liabilities?'

'Er . . . yes. More than enough, I believe. But are you sure you want to do this, Lady Eleanor? The house is in your sole name, you know. It is your property,' he stressed.

'And Joss is my husband,' Nell responded fiercely.

Something almost approaching a smile touched his mouth.

'Very well. There'll be certain arrangements we'll need to make. I suggest you go home now, and we'll be in touch.'

'And Joss won't be declared bankrupt,' Nell pressed.

'I think I can safely assure you of that . . .' He paused and smiled again, and said gently, 'You must love your husband a great deal, Lady Eleanor.'

Nell averted her head. 'Yes,' she agreed huskily. 'I do.'

She refused a cup of coffee and thanked him for his time. He escorted her off the bank's premises and then went back to his office and picked up his intercom.

'Get me Joss Wycliffe at that New York number he left for us, will you, Jane?'

'Ah, Joss,' he said genially some ten mintues later when his secretary put the call through. 'I've just had a most extraordinary interview with your wife.'

Joss arrived home without warning, just after Nell had finished toying with a meal she didn't really want. She was in the library reading the *Financial Times,* trying to look for some clue as to what had actually happened, but there was no mention of Joss's name.

She stood up uncertainly as he opened the door, and then gasped out his name in surprise as he covered the distance between them and picked her up in his arms, kissing her fiercely.

It was a dream . . a mirage . . . it had to be, but that didn't stop her from responding ardently to the urgent pressure of his mouth, or from pressing herself eagerly against the aroused hardness of his body.

'Just one question, Nell,' he told her, releasing

her mouth. 'Despite everything I've said and done
. . . depsite what's happened between us . . . Could
you . . . do you love me?'

Her face gave her away.

'Oh, God, Nell,' he swore thickly. '*Why* haven't
you said so? Why did you let me think you didn't
care?'

'Because I thought that was what you wanted,'
she told him, raising bemused eyes to his
face.

He had lost weight and looked far more
vulnerable human than she had ever seen him look
before. She touched his jaw with fingers that shook a
little, gasping softly when he caught hold of her wrist
and lifted her palm to his mouth, placing a kiss in its
cupped hollow.

'What I wanted . . . what I still want is you. Not
the public Lady Eleanor, Nell, but the real you. I've
glimpsed her once or twice. I've even managed to
warm the coldness of my life in the heat of her
compassion. I used to watch you with your
grandfather and envy him.'

He felt her start and smiled grimly.

'Didn't you guess how I felt? He did, and in his
last months he took pity on me and told me that
when he was gone, he hoped I would marry you and
take care of you and Easterhay.'

'But you told me you were marrying me for the
title.'

'It was the best excuse I could find. I was
desperately afraid I was going to lose you to
Williams.'

'David? But, Joss, how could you have thought
that?'

'Very easily. Men as deeply and hopelessly in love

as I was then are possessive and jealous. Besides, Grania told me she thought you would marry him. Do you remember? She came home the weekend before I proposed to you. She mentioned it then, when she was asking for an advance on her allowance.'

'But Grania knew how I felt about you. She guessed from something I said. She warned me that you'd never look twice at someone like me, and I thought she was right. Oh, Joss, how can you love me? I'm not beautiful, or sophisticated. I . . .'

'You are beautiful,' he corrected her huskily, 'and not just physically. How many girls of your age would have given up their independence, as you did, to nurse a bad-tempered old man?

'I fell in love with Cheshire when I spent a few days here on business. Up until then I'd lived in London. So I bought myself a house here, never dreaming that it was going to lead to the most painful and self-destructive period of my life. When I first moved up here, I considered myself impervious to dangers like falling in love. The way I'd grown up had toughened me, Nell, and clawing my way up the ladder via commodity-dealing finished off the process.

'If I ever thought about marriage . . . about sharing my life with one person, it was with a sense of contempt for those people I knew who were idiotic enough to commit themselves in such a way.

'And then I met you, and you turned every belief I had upside-down. At first I couldn't believe what I was feeling. How could I have fallen in love with a woman who would barely bring herself to say my name, who turned her head and refused to look at me every time we met, who disappeared like woodsmoke in the sunlight whenever I tried to pin her down?'

'I thought you came here to see Gramps,' Nell told him painfully. 'I thought that if I was always hanging around you would guess how I felt about you and . . . and be amused by it . . .'

'Oh, Nell . . . what idiots we've both been.'

The words were muffled against her hair as he held her.

'When you made love to me that first time . . . I wanted to tell you then. I thought you'd probably guessed . . . and then when Fiona came round and told me that you'd told her what had happened and that you'd had to force yourself to make love to me . . .'

He felt the shudder that convulsed her, and tightened his hold of her slender body.

'She was lying to you,' he told her gruffly. 'She must have guessed what had happened. I think I rather gave the game away that morning by acting like a lovesick eighteen-year-old. I telephoned you . . .'

Nell shook her head, silencing him, and said quietly, 'No—you asked Fiona to telephone me.'

She saw comprehension dawn in the gold eyes, 'That bitch! he swore bitterly. 'It's just as well she's already left the country.'

'She loved you, Joss,' Nell told him, prepared to make allowances for the other woman now that she herself was so gloriously secure in Joss's love.

'Not me,' he told her, correcting her. 'It was my money she loved. Do you know that you're the first person in my entire life who's ever wanted to do something for me . . . who's ever been prepared to make a sacrifice for me —and such a sacrifice, Nell.'

He looked down at her and she could have sworn it was tears that made his eyes glitter.

'Would you really have done that? Mortgaged this place as security?'

'Ten times over,' she assured him truthfully. 'Tell me the truth, Joss. How bad are things for you financially? It doesn't matter,' she added quickly as he tensed. 'Whatever happens . . .'

'Oh, Nell, Nell. Fiona lied to you. I'm nowhere near the edge of bankruptcy. It's true that I could have lost a great deal of money on a recent deal, but I didn't, I made a lot instead. That's what being a successful commodity-broker is all about. But do you know something—I'm getting rather tired of the cut and thrust of dealing. They do say that you begin to lose your edge once you're over thirty, and I'm five years beyond that. What would you say if I told you I was considering retiring and concentrating on building up the estate . . . on becoming something of a "gentleman farmer" . . .?'

'Oh Joss . . .'

The delight in her face showed him exactly what she felt, the parted warmth of her mouth too much temptation for him to even try to resist.

It was a long time before he stopped kissing her, and then Nell asked breathlessly, 'But Fiona . . . why on earth did she lie to me like that? She must have known I'd find out.'

'I don't think she thought that far ahead. She wanted to lash out and hurt us . . . . hurt me. While I was in New York she turned up totally unexpectedly at my hotel suite and announced that she thought it was time she and I became lovers. I told her then that there was only one woman I wanted to make love to and that was my wife. I should have

have guessed then that she'd want to retaliate, but she caught me off guard, at a time when I couldn't get away from the deal I was doing, and when all I wanted to do . . . when all I ached to do was to be with you, so consequently I was far less tactful then perhaps I should have been . . .'

'She told me you'd been to see your solicitor about a divorce.'

'Oh, Nell, she lied to you. There was no way I would have let you go, even if my conscience was telling me that was exactly what I should do. You see, I thought that once I'd made love to you I'd be able to break through your barriers; that if we could share physical pleasure, in time you might come to feel an emotional bond with me. What I didn't bargain for was how guilty making love to you made me feel. I suddenly realised exactly what I was doing to you; that by forcing you into marriage with me, I'd stolen from you your right to fall in love.'

'But I'd already fallen in love,' Nell told him huskily, and then added, 'Joss, you haven't made love to me once since our wedding night.'

'Because I dared not. I couldn't without telling you how much I loved you, and I was terrified that if I did that, I'd frighten you off for ever. The title . . . the house . . . none of it mattered, Nell. It was just you. Did you really think I was so shallow? If I'd just wanted a title for my son, there were other women I could have married.' His hands cupped her face, his thumb tracing the curve of her bottom lip and then probing the trembling corner of her mouth, parting her lips so that she felt the roughness of his flesh against their softness. She drew a shaky breath, intending to tell him how much she loved him, but the words were lost as he bent his head and said slowly, 'Oh, God, Nell, if you only knew how I've dreamed of doing this . . . and this . . .' He kissed her slowly, and then added rawly, 'Of making love to you until you cried out my name with pleasure . . . Ah, Nell . . .'

She felt him tremble as she reached up and kissed him, a little uncertainly at first and then with growing confidence as she felt his unchecked response.

When they broke apart, she said breathlessly, 'I hope you won't need champagne to make love to me tonight, because I don't think we've got any.'

There was a silence while he looked at her in a way that made her body burn, and then he said quietly, 'That wasn't so that I could make love to you. It was so that I wouldn't. Only, when I saw you in that nightdress, I knew I was wasting my time . . . Nell, do you think a husband suffering from jet-lag might quite reasonably go to bed at four o'clock in the afternoon?'

'It's Mrs Booth's afternoon off,' Nell told him obliquely, willingly letting him draw her out into the hall and up the stairs to their room.

'Oh, Nell, she's so beautiful. I'd forgotten how adorable new babies are. It makes me feel quite broody. What about Joss, though? I thought he'd set his heart on a boy.'

'Joss spoils her to death,' Nell grinned as she and Liz both looked down at the baby in her ribbon-festooned crib.

'I heard that,' Joss announced, coming into the nursery in time to hear Nell's comment, and then unwittingly confirming what Nell had just said by bending over the crib and crooning nonsense over his sleeping daughter.

'See, I told you,' Nell said wryly. 'I'm barely allowed to touch her.'

Picking up the baby and cradling her against his shoulder, Joss turned to look at her and said softly, 'Nell, as much as I love our daughter, I could never love her as much as I do her mother.'

'Hey, you two, break it up,' Liz demanded. 'You're making me feel quite weepy, and in front of your daughter, too . . . Joss, if you and Nell want to be alone . . .'

'An excellent suggestion,' Joss agreed, ignoring Nell's protest to grin at Liz, and hand over the soon-to-be christened Charlotte Louise to her doting godmother—to—be.

'Why don't Nell and I leave you to become acquainted with your god-daughter to be, while I become re-acquainted with my wife?'

'Joss, what on earth must Liz be thinking?' Nell protested huskily as Joss deftly whisked her out of the nursery and closed the door firmly behind them, silencing Liz's amused laughter.

'Oh, I expect she thinks I want to make love to my wife, and do you know something?' he murmured against her ear, taking her in his arms. 'She's quite right.'

Half an hour later, when Robert walked into the nursery in search of his wife and hosts, he asked Liz curiously, 'What's happened to Nell and Joss?'

'Umm . . . that, I believe, is a rather indelicate question.' She grinned up at him, and said thought-fully, 'Robert, she's adorable, isn't she? Now that Lucy is two . . .'

'Another baby? God, Liz what are you trying to do to me? Do you realise that would mean we have *four* children? It's positively indecent . . .'

'Ah, yes, but think what it would do for your image,' she teased him.

In their bedroom, sunlight fell across the bed, bathing Nell's body in its warmth.

'We really ought to go downstairs,' she protested drowsily as Joss drew her down against him.

'Later . . .' Joss told her, and, looking into the golden heat of his eyes, Nell didn't demur.

# Especially for you, Christmas from
# HARLEQUIN HISTORICALS

An enchanting collection of three Christmas
stories by some of your favorite authors captures
the spirit of the season in the 1800s

## TUMBLEWEED CHRISTMAS by Kristin James

A "Bah, humbug" Texas rancher meets his match in his
new housekeeper, a woman determined to bring the spirit
of a Tumbleweed Christmas into his life—and love into
his heart.

## A CINDERELLA CHRISTMAS by Lucy Elliot

The perfect granddaughter, sister and aunt, Mary Hillyer
seemed destined for spinsterhood until Jack Gates arrived
to discover a woman with dreams and passions that were
meant to be shared during a Cinderella Christmas.

## HOME FOR CHRISTMAS
## by Heather Graham Pozzessere

The magic of the season brings peace Home For
Christmas when a Yankee captain and a Southern heiress
fall in love during the Civil War.

HIST-XMAS-1R

# HARLEQUIN'S "BIG WIN"
## SWEEPSTAKES RULES & REGULATIONS
### NO PURCHASE NECESSARY TO ENTER OR RECEIVE A PRIZE

1. To enter and join the Harlequin Reader Service, scratch off the pink metallic strips on all your BIG WIN tickets #1-#6. This will reveal the values for each sweepstakes entry number, the number of free books you will receive and your free bonus gift as part of our Reader Service. If you do not wish to take advantage of our introduction to the Harlequin Reader Service but wish to enter the Sweepstakes only, scratch off the pink metallic strips on your BIG WIN tickets #1-#4 only. To enter, return your entire sheet of tickets intact. Incomplete and/or inaccurate entries are not eligible for that section or section(s) of prizes. Not responsible for mutilated or unreadable entries or inadvertent printing errors. Mechanically reproduced entries are null and void.

2. Either way your unique Sweepstakes numbers will be compared against the list of winning numbers generated at random by the computer. In the event that all prizes are not claimed, random drawings will be held from all entries received from all presentations to award all unclaimed prizes. All cash prizes are payable in U.S. funds. This is in addition to any free, surprise or mystery gifts that might be offered. The following prizes are awarded in this sweepstakes: *Grand Prize (1) $1,000,000; First Prize (1) $35,000; Second Prize (1) $10,000; Third Prize (3) $5,000; Fourth Prize (10) $1,000; Fifth Prize (25) $500; Sixth Prize (5000)$5.

    *This Sweepstakes contains a Grand Prize offering of a $1,000,000 annuity. Winner may elect to receive $25,000 a year for 40 years without interest totalling $1,000,000 or $350,000 in one cash payment. Entrants may cancel Reader Service at any time without cost or obligation to buy (see details in center insert card).

3. Extra Bonus Prize: This presentation offers two extra bonus prizes valued at $30,000 each to be awarded in a random drawing from all entries received.

4. Versions of this Sweepstakes with different graphics will be offered in other mailings or at retail outlets by Torstar Corp. and its affiliates. This promotion is being conducted under the supervision of Marden-Kane, Inc., an independent judging organization. By entering this Sweepstakes, each entrant accepts and agrees to be bound by these rules and the decisions of the judges, which shall be final and binding. Odds of winning in the random drawing are dependent upon the total number of entries received. Taxes, if any, are the sole responsibility of the winners. Prizes are non-transferable. All entries must be received by March 31, 1990. The drawing will take place on or about April 30, 1990 at the offices of Marden-Kane, Inc., Lake Success, NY.

5. This offer is open to residents of the U.S., the United Kingdom and Canada, 18 years or older except employees of Torstar Corp., its affiliates, subsidiaries, Marden-Kane, Inc. and all other agencies and persons connected with conducting this Sweepstakes. All Federal, State and local laws apply. Void wherever prohibited or restricted by law.

6. Winners will be notified by mail and may be required to execute an affidavit of eligibility and release that must be returned within 14 days after notification. Canadian winners will be required to answer a skill-testing question. Winners consent to the use of their name, photograph and/or likeness for advertising and publicity in conjunction with this and similar promotions without additional compensation.

7 For a list of our most current major prize winners, send a stamped, self-addressed envelope to: WINNERS LIST c/o MARDEN-KANE, INC., P.O. BOX 701, SAYREVILLE, NJ 08871.

---

If Sweepstakes entry form is missing, please print your name and address on a 3" × 5" piece of plain paper and send to:

| In the U.S. | In Canada |
|---|---|
| Harlequin's "BIG WIN" Sweepstakes | Harlequin's "BIG WIN" Sweepstakes |
| 901 Fuhrmann Blvd. | P.O. Box 609 |
| Box 1867 | Fort Erie, Ontario |
| Buffalo, NY 14269-1867 | L2A 5X3 |

© 1989 Harlequin Enterprises Limited   Printed in the U.S.A.                    LTY-H119

Wonderful, luxurious gifts can be yours with proofs-of-purchase from any specially marked "Indulge A Little" Harlequin or Silhouette book with the Offer Certificate properly completed, plus a check or money order (do not send cash) to cover postage and handling payable to Harlequin/Silhouette "Indulge A Little, Give A Lot" Offer. We will send you the specified gift.

**Mail-in-Offer**

| Item | **OFFER CERTIFICATE** | | | |
|---|---|---|---|---|
| | A. Collector's Doll | B. Soaps in a Basket | C. Potpourri Sachet | D. Scented Hangers |
| # of Proofs-of -Purchase | 18 | 12 | 6 | 4 |
| Postage & Handling | $3.25 | $2.75 | $2.25 | $2.00 |
| Check One | | | | |

Name _____

Address _____ Apt. # _____

City _____ State _____ Zip _____

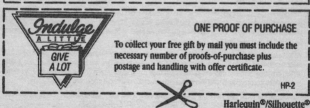

**ONE PROOF OF PURCHASE**

To collect your free gift by mail you must include the necessary number of proofs-of-purchase plus postage and handling with offer certificate.

HP-2

Harlequin®/Silhouette®

Mail this certificate, designated number of proofs-of-purchase and check or money order for postage and handling to:

INDULGE A LITTLE
P.O. Box 9055
Buffalo, N.Y. 14269-9055